PHANTOM of the AUDITORIUM

GOOSEBUMPS HorrorLand™

Also Available from Scholastic Audio Books

GOOSEBUMPS®
HALL OF HORRORS

GOOSEBUMPS®
NOW WITH BONUS FEATURES!

NIGHT OF THE LIVING DUMMY
DEEP TROUBLE
MONSTER BLOOD
THE HAUNTED MASK
ONE DAY AT HORRORLAND
THE CURSE OF THE MUMMY'S TOMB
BE CAREFUL WHAT YOU WISH FOR
SAY CHEESE AND DIE!
THE HORROR AT CAMP JELLYJAM
HOW I GOT MY SHRUNKEN HEAD
THE WEREWOLF OF FEVER SWAMP
A NIGHT IN TERROR TOWER
WELCOME TO DEAD HOUSE
WELCOME TO CAMP NIGHTMARE
GHOST BEACH
THE SCARECROW WALKS AT MIDNIGHT
YOU CAN'T SCARE ME!
RETURN OF THE MUMMY
REVENGE OF THE LAWN GNOMES
PHANTOM OF THE AUDITORIUM

Goosebumps®

PHANTOM of the AUDITORIUM

R.L. STINE

SCHOLASTIC INC.

NEW YORK TORONTO LONDON AUCKLAND
SYDNEY MEXICO CITY NEW DELHI HONG KONG

No part of this publication may be reproduced, stored in a retrieval system, or transmitted in any form or by any means, electronic, mechanical, photocopying, recording, or otherwise, without written permission of the publisher. For information regarding permission, write to Scholastic Inc., Attention: Permissions Department, 557 Broadway, New York, NY 10012.

ISBN 978-0-545-29836-0

Goosebumps book series created by Parachute Press, Inc.
Copyright © 1994 by Scholastic Inc.

All rights reserved. Published by Scholastic Inc., *Publishers since 1920.* SCHOLASTIC, GOOSEBUMPS, GOOSEBUMPS HORRORLAND, and associated logos are trademarks and/or registered trademarks of Scholastic Inc.

12 11 10 9 8 7 6 5 4 3 2 1   11 12 13 14 15 16/0

Printed in the U.S.A.   40
First printing, June 2011

"Behind the Screams" bonus material by Gabrielle S. Balkan

A mysterious phantom haunted our school.

No one ever saw him. No one knew where he lived.

But he haunted our school for more than seventy years.

My best friend, Zeke, and I were the ones who found him. We found him while we were doing a school play about a phantom.

Our teacher told us that the play was cursed, but we didn't believe her. We thought it was all just a big joke.

But when I saw the Phantom for myself, I knew it was no joke. It was all true. Every bit of it.

The night we found the Phantom was the scariest night of our lives!

But I should start at the beginning.

My name is Brooke Rodgers, and I'm in the sixth grade at Woods Mill Middle School.

Zeke Matthews is my best friend. A lot of the other girls think it's weird that my best friend is a boy, but I don't care. Zeke is cooler and funnier than any girls I know. He is also a big horror movie fan, like me.

Zeke and I have been best friends for nine years. We know just about everything about each other. For instance, I know that Zeke still wears Kermit the Frog pajamas!

He hates it when I tell people that. His face always turns a bright shade of red. Then his freckles stand out even more.

Zeke hates his freckles almost as much as I hate my glasses. I don't know why he's so hung up over a couple of freckles. After a while, you hardly even notice them. And in the summer when he gets tan, they practically disappear altogether.

I wish my glasses could disappear. They make me look so nerdy. But if I don't wear them, I walk into walls!

Some girls at school think Zeke is cute. I never think about him that way. I guess it's because I've known him for nearly my entire life. Ever since our moms met in their bowling league and discovered they lived on the same street.

The excitement about the Phantom started a couple of Fridays ago. School had ended for the day, and I was trying to get my locker open. I pushed my hair off my face and turned the combination dial. The stupid lock always jams, and it drives me crazy.

After trying the combination four times, I finally got it open. I threw my books inside and slammed the door shut. No way was I dragging home any textbooks over the weekend. As of right this second, I was on vacation! Two whole days of no school.

Excellent.

Before I could turn around, a fist came whizzing by my ear and punched my locker with a loud *bang*!

"What's up, Brookie?" a voice called from behind me. "No homework this weekend?"

I didn't have to turn around to know who it was. Only one person in the whole world can ever get away with calling me Brookie.

I turned around to see Zeke's dopey grin. His blond hair, which was really long in the front and very short — almost shaved — in the back, fell over one eye.

I smiled, then stuck my tongue out at him.

"Real mature, Brookie," he muttered.

Then I flipped my eyelids up so they stayed that way. It's a really gross talent I have that usually makes people scream and gag.

Zeke didn't bat an eye. He has seen my eyelid trick at least a zillion times.

"Nope, no homework!" I replied. "No books. No nothing. I'm totally free this weekend."

Then I got a great idea. "Hey, Zeke," I said, "do you think Rich can take us to see the *Creature* festival tomorrow?"

I was dying to see the three *Creature* movies playing at the Cineplex. One was supposed to be in 3–D! Zeke and I go to scary movies all the time just to laugh at the scary parts. We have nerves of steel. We never get scared.

"Maybe," Zeke answered, brushing his hair away from his face. "But Rich is grounded. He can't use the car for a week."

Rich is Zeke's older brother. He spends most of his life being grounded.

Zeke shifted his backpack onto his shoulder. "Forget about the *Creature* festival, Brooke. Aren't you forgetting something?" He narrowed his eyes at me. "Something big?"

I scrunched up my nose. Forgetting something? I couldn't think of a thing. "What?" I asked finally.

"Come on, Brookie! Think!"

I really had no idea what Zeke was talking about. I pulled my long hair into a ponytail and tied it together with the scrunchie that was on my wrist.

I always wear a scrunchie on each wrist. I like to be prepared. You never know when you're going to need a scrunchie.

"Really, Zeke, I don't know," I said, making a tight ponytail. "Why don't you just tell me?"

And that's when it hit me. "The cast list!" I yelled, slapping my forehead. How could I have forgotten? Zeke and I had been waiting two long weeks to find out if we got parts in the school play.

"Come on! Let's check it out!" I grabbed hold of Zeke's flannel shirtsleeve. And I pulled him all the way to the auditorium.

Zeke and I had both tried out for the play. Last year, we had small parts in the musical *Guys and Dolls*. Ms. Walker, our teacher, told us that the play this year was going to be scary.

That's all Zeke and I had to hear. We *had* to be in this play!

We found a big crowd of kids at the bulletin board. They were all trying to read the cast list at once.

I was so nervous! "I can't look, Zeke!" I cried. "You check, okay?"

"Yeah, no prob —"

"Wait! I'll do it!" I yelled, changing my mind. I do that a lot. Zeke says it drives him crazy.

I took a deep breath and pushed through the crowd of kids. Biting my left thumbnail, I crossed the fingers on my right hand and stared up at the list.

But when I saw what was posted up there, I nearly bit off my whole thumb!

Tacked on the board beside the cast list was a sign:

ATTENTION BROOKE RODGERS: PLEASE REPORT TO
MR. LEVY'S OFFICE. YOU HAVE BEEN SUSPENDED
FROM SCHOOL.

Suspended?

I gasped in shock.

Had Mr. Levy found out that I was the one who let the gerbil loose in the teachers' lounge?

Suspended.

I felt sick to my stomach. My parents were going to be so horrified.

Then I heard giggling.

I spun around to find Zeke laughing his head off. Other kids were laughing, too.

I stared angrily at Zeke. "Did you put that sign up?"

"Of course!" he replied, laughing even harder.

He has a sick sense of humor.

"I didn't believe it for a second," I lied.

I turned back to the board to read the cast list. I had to read the list three times. I couldn't believe what I saw. "Zeke!" I shouted over the other kids' heads. "You and I — we're the stars!"

Zeke's mouth dropped open in surprise. Then he grinned at me. "Yeah. For sure," he muttered, rolling his eyes.

"No. Really!" I cried. "We got the two biggest parts! Come check it out for yourself! You got the part of the Phantom!"

"No way!" Zeke still didn't believe me.

"She's telling the truth, Zeke," a girl behind me said. Tina Powell, a seventh-grader, pushed through the crowd.

I always get the feeling that Tina Powell doesn't like me very much. I have no idea why. I hardly even know her. But she always seems to be frowning at me. Like I have a piece of spinach caught in my teeth or something.

"Let me see that list!" Zeke demanded, pushing past everyone. "Wow! I *did* get the starring part!"

"I'm going to be Esmerelda," I read. "I wonder who Esmerelda is. Hey, maybe she's the Phantom's crazy old stepmother, or maybe she's the headless wife who comes back from the dead to —"

"Give it a rest, Brooke," Tina said, frowning at me. "Esmerelda is just the daughter of some guy who owns the theater." She said it as if Esmerelda were a nothing part.

"Uh, what part did you get, Tina?" I asked.

Tina shifted uncomfortably. A few other kids turned to hear her reply.

"I'm *your* understudy!" she muttered, staring down at the floor. "So if you get sick or something and you can't be in the show, I'll play the part of Esmerelda.

"I'm also in charge of all the scenery!" she boasted.

I wanted to say something mean and nasty, something to put Miss High-and-Mighty Tina Powell in her place in front of everybody. But I couldn't think of anything.

I'm not a mean, nasty person. And it's hard to think of mean, nasty things to say — even when I want to.

So I decided to ignore her. I was too excited about the play to let Tina Powell get to me.

I pulled on my denim jacket and swung my backpack over my shoulder. "Come on, Phantom," I said to Zeke. "Let's go haunt the neighborhood!"

On Monday afternoon, we started rehearsing the play. Ms. Walker was in charge.

She stood us on the stage in the auditorium, staring down at us. She clutched a tall stack of scripts in her arms.

Ms. Walker has curly red hair and pretty green eyes. She is very skinny, as skinny as a pencil. She is a very good teacher — a little too strict. But a good teacher.

Zeke and I chose two seats next to each other in the third row. I glanced around at the other kids. Everyone was talking. Everyone seemed really excited.

"Do you know what this play is about?" Corey Sklar asked me. He was playing my father. I mean, Esmerelda's father. Corey has chestnut-brown hair like me. And he also wears glasses. Maybe that's why we were playing relatives.

"Beats me," I answered him with a shrug. "Nobody knows what the play is about. I just know it's supposed to be scary."

"I know what it's about!" Tina Powell announced loudly.

I turned around in my seat. "How do you know?" I demanded. "Ms. Walker hasn't passed out the scripts yet."

"My great-grandfather went to Woods Mill Middle School a long, long time ago. He told me all about *The Phantom*," Tina bragged.

I started to tell Tina that nobody cared about her great-grandfather's dumb story. But then she added, "He also told me about the *curse* on the play!"

That shut everyone up. Even me.

Even Ms. Walker was listening now.

Zeke nudged me, his eyes wide with excitement. "A curse?" he whispered happily. "Cool!"

I nodded. "Very cool," I muttered.

"My great-grandfather told me a really scary story about this play," Tina continued. "And he told me about a phantom in the school. A real phantom who —"

"Tina!" Ms. Walker interrupted, stepping to the front of the stage. She peered down sharply at Tina. "I really don't think you should tell that story today."

"Huh? Why not?" I cried.

"Yeah. Why not?" Zeke joined in.

"I don't think this is a good time to listen to scary stories that may not be true," Ms. Walker replied sternly. "Today I'm going to pass out the scripts, and —"

"Do you *know* the story?" Tina demanded.

"Yes, I've heard it," Ms. Walker told her. "But I wish you would keep it to yourself, Tina. It's a very scary story. Very upsetting. And I really don't think —"

"Tell us! Tell us! Tell us!" Zeke started to chant.

And, instantly, we were all grinning up at our teacher and chanting loudly: "Tell us! Tell us! Tell us!"

Why didn't Ms. Walker want us to hear the story? I wondered.

How scary could it be?

"Tell us! Tell us! Tell us!" we all continued to chant.

Ms. Walker raised both hands for us to be silent.

But that only made us stamp our feet in time to our chanting.

"Tell us! Tell us! Tell us!"

"Okay!" she shouted finally. "Okay, I'll tell you the story. But, remember — it's just a story. I don't want you to get too scared."

"You can't scare *us*!" Zeke cried.

Everyone laughed. But I was staring hard at Ms. Walker. I could see that she really didn't want us to know this story.

Ms. Walker always said we could talk about anything we wanted to with her. I began to wonder why she didn't want to talk about the Phantom.

"The story starts seventy-two years ago," Ms. Walker began, "the year Woods Mill Middle

School was first built. I guess Tina's great-grandfather was a student here that year."

"Yes, he was," Tina called out. "He was in the first class that went to this school. He told me there were only twenty-five kids in the whole school."

Ms. Walker crossed her skinny arms over the front of her yellow sweater and continued her story. "The students wanted to put on a play. A boy was hunting around in the basement of the old Woods Mill Library. He found a script down there. It was called *The Phantom*.

"It was a very scary play about a girl who is kidnapped by a mysterious phantom. The boy showed it to his teacher. The teacher decided it would be fun to perform the play. It would be a grand production with the best scary special effects they could create."

Zeke and I exchanged excited glances. The play had special effects! We loved special effects!

"Rehearsals for *The Phantom* began," Ms. Walker continued. "The boy who had discovered the play at the library won the lead role of the Phantom."

Everybody turned to look at Zeke. He smiled proudly, as if he had something to do with it.

"They practiced the play after school every day," Ms. Walker continued. "Everyone was having a really good time. Everyone was working really hard to make it a good play. It was all going smoothly, until — until —"

She hesitated.

"Tell us!" I called out loudly.

"Tell us! Tell us!" a few kids started chanting again.

"I want you all to remember this is just a story," Ms. Walker said again. "There's no proof that it ever happened."

We all nodded.

Ms. Walker cleared her throat, then continued. "On the night of the play, the kids were all in costume. Parents and friends filled the auditorium. *This* auditorium. The kids were really excited and nervous.

"Their teacher called them together to give them a pep talk. The play was about to start. But to everyone's surprise, the boy playing the Phantom was nowhere to be found."

Ms. Walker began pacing back and forth on the stage as she continued the story. "They called to him. They looked for him backstage. But they couldn't find the Phantom, the star of the show.

"They spread out. They searched everywhere. But they couldn't find him. The boy had vanished.

"They searched for an hour," Ms. Walker continued. "Everyone was so upset, so frightened. Especially the boy's parents.

"Finally, the teacher stepped out onstage to announce that the play could not go on. But before she could speak, a horrible scream rang out over the auditorium."

Ms. Walker stopped pacing. "It was a frightening scream. People said it was like an animal howl.

"The teacher ran toward the sound. She called to the boy. But now there was only silence. A heavy silence. No more screams.

"Once again, the entire school was searched. But the boy was never found."

Ms. Walker swallowed hard.

We were all silent. No one even breathed!

"He was never seen again," she repeated. "I guess you could say that the Phantom became a *real* phantom. He just disappeared. And the play was never performed."

She stopped pacing and stared out at us. Her eyes moved from seat to seat.

"Weird," someone behind me murmured.

"Do you think it's true?" I heard a boy whisper.

And then, beside me, Corey Sklar let out a gasp. "Oh, no!" he cried, pointing to the side door. "There he is! There's the Phantom!"

I turned — along with everyone else — and saw the hideous face of the Phantom, grinning at us from the doorway.

Corey Sklar screamed.

A lot of kids screamed. I think even Tina screamed.

The Phantom's face was twisted in an ugly grin. His bright red hair stood straight up on his head. One eyeball bulged out from its socket. Black stitches covered a deep scar that ran all the way down the side of his face.

"BOO!" the Phantom yelled, bursting into the aisle.

More screams.

I just laughed. I knew it was Zeke.

I had seen him wear that dumb mask before. He kept it in his book bag in case he needed it.

"Zeke, give us a break!" I called.

He pulled the mask off by the hair. His face was red underneath it. Zeke grinned at everyone. He knew he had just pulled off a really good joke.

Kids were laughing now.

Someone threw an empty milk container at Zeke. Another kid tried to trip Zeke as he headed back to his seat.

"Very funny, Zeke," Ms. Walker said, rolling her eyes. "I hope we won't have any more visits from the Phantom!"

Zeke dropped back into the seat next to me. "Why did you scare everyone like that?" I whispered.

"Felt like it." Zeke grinned back at me.

"So, will we be the first kids to perform this play?" Corey asked Ms. Walker.

Our teacher nodded. "Yes, we will. After the boy disappeared seventy-two years ago, the school decided to destroy all the scripts and the scenery. But one copy of the script was kept, locked up in the school vault for all these years. And now *we're* going to perform *The Phantom* for the first time!"

Kids started talking excitedly. It took Ms. Walker a while to quiet us down.

"Now listen," she said, putting her hands on her pencil-thin waist. "This was just a story. An old school legend. I'll bet even Tina's great-grandfather will tell you that it isn't true. I only told it to put you all in a horror mood."

"But what about the curse?" I shouted up to her. "Tina said there was a curse!"

"Yes," Tina called out. "My great-grandfather said the play is cursed. The Phantom won't let anyone perform it. Great-grandpa says the Phantom is still here in the school. The Phantom has been haunting the school for over seventy years! But no one has ever seen him."

"Excellent!" Zeke declared, his eyes lighting up.

Some kids laughed. Some kids looked kind of uncomfortable. Kind of scared.

"I told you, it's just a story," Ms. Walker said. "Now, let's get down to business, okay? Who wants to help me pass the scripts out? I've made a copy for each of you. I want you to take them home and begin studying your parts."

Zeke and I practically fell over each other running up to the stage to help Ms. Walker. She handed us each a stack of scripts. We climbed back down and started to hand them out. When I came to Corey, he pulled his hand back. "Wh-what if the curse is true?" he called up to Ms. Walker.

"Corey, please," she insisted. "Enough talk about the Phantom and the curse, okay? We have a lot of work to do, and —"

She didn't finish.

Instead, she screamed.

I turned back to the stage, where Ms. Walker had been standing a second before.

She was gone.

She had vanished into thin air.

The scripts fell from my hands.

I turned and made a dash for the stage. I heard kids shouting and crying out in surprise.

"She just disappeared!" I heard Corey utter.

"But that's *impossible*!" a girl shrieked.

Zeke and I scrambled onstage together. "Ms. Walker — where are you?" I called. "Ms. Walker?"

Silence.

"Ms. Walker? Can you hear me?" Zeke called.

Then I heard Ms. Walker's faint cry for help. "I'm down here!" she called.

"Down where?" Zeke cried.

"Down here!"

Down below the stage? That's where her voice seemed to be coming from.

"Help me up!" Ms. Walker called again.

What's going on here? I wondered. *How come we can hear her, but we can't see her?*

19

I was the first to spot the big square hole in the stage. Zeke and the other kids gathered around it. I stepped to the edge of the opening and peered down.

Ms. Walker stared up at me. She was standing on a small square platform, five or six feet below the stage. "You'll have to raise the platform," she said.

"How do we bring it up?" Zeke asked.

"Press that peg. Over there on the stage," Ms. Walker instructed. She pointed to a small wooden peg to the right of the trapdoor.

"Got it!" Zeke cried. He pushed down the peg. We heard a clanking sound. Then a grinding sound. Then a groaning sound.

Slowly, the platform came rising up. Ms. Walker stepped off the platform. She grinned at us and brushed off the back of her blue slacks. "I forgot about the trapdoor," she said. "I could have broken a leg or something. But I think I'm okay."

We all gathered around. Zeke dropped down on his hands and knees, staring at the trapdoor.

"I forgot to mention the best part about this play," Ms. Walker told us. "This trapdoor was built for the first production of *The Phantom*. It was totally forgotten. It's never been used in a school play — until now!"

My mouth dropped open. A trapdoor! How awesome!

Ms. Walker reached down and tugged Zeke back from the opening. "Careful. You'll fall," she said. "I lowered the platform earlier. I forgot it was still down."

Zeke climbed to his feet. I could see he was really interested in the trapdoor.

"When *The Phantom* was first supposed to be performed," Ms. Walker told us, "the school had this trapdoor built so that the Phantom could disappear or rise up from below. Back then, it was a very impressive special effect."

I turned my eyes to Zeke. He seemed about to explode with excitement. "Am I the only one who gets to use it in the play?" he asked eagerly. "Can I try it now? Please?"

"Not yet, Zeke," Ms. Walker replied firmly. "I still need to have it checked out for safety reasons. Until it has been checked, I don't want anybody fooling with the trapdoor."

Zeke was already back on his hands and knees, inspecting the trapdoor.

Ms. Walker cleared her throat loudly. "Is that understood? Zeke?" she asked.

Zeke glanced up. He sighed. "Yes, Ms. Walker," he muttered.

"Good," Ms. Walker said. "Now let's get back to our seats. I'd like to read through the play once before we leave today. Just to give you an idea of the story and the characters."

We returned to our seats. Zeke's expression caught my eye. I'd seen that look on his face before. His forehead was wrinkled, and his left eyebrow was up. I could tell he was deep in thought.

It took more than an hour to read through the play. *The Phantom* was really scary.

It was about a man named Carlo who owns a very old theater where plays and concerts are performed. Carlo thinks his theater is haunted.

It turns out that there really is a phantom living in the basement. His face is scarred. He looks like a monster. So he wears a mask. But Carlo's daughter, Esmerelda, falls in love with the Phantom. She plans to run away with him. But her handsome boyfriend, Eric, finds out.

Eric is in love with Esmerelda. He tracks down the Phantom in his secret home in a dark passage far beneath the theater. They fight. And Eric kills the Phantom.

This breaks Esmerelda's heart. She runs away, never to be seen again. And the Phantom survives as a ghost. He will haunt the theater forever.

Pretty dramatic, huh?

I think we all enjoyed reading through the play. We could see that it was going to be a lot of fun to perform.

When I read my lines as Esmerelda, I tried to picture what it would be like to be in costume, saying the lines onstage. Once, I glanced back and saw Tina mouthing my lines silently to herself.

She stopped when she caught me watching her. She frowned at me the way she always does.

Tina is totally jealous, I told myself. *She really wants to be Esmerelda.*

For a moment, I felt bad for Tina. I didn't like Tina very much. But I didn't want her to *hate* me because I had the part she wanted to play.

But I didn't have much time to think about Tina. I had a lot of lines to read. Esmerelda was onstage a lot in this play. It was a really big part.

When we finally finished reading the play, we all clapped and cheered.

"Okay. Go home, everyone," Ms. Walker instructed, waving us to the door. "Start learning your parts. We'll meet again tomorrow."

As I began to follow the other kids to the door, I felt a hand pull me back. I turned to find Zeke pulling me behind a wide concrete beam.

"Zeke — what are you doing?" I demanded.

He raised a finger to his lips. "*Shhhh.*" His eyes were really excited. "Let them all go," he whispered.

I peeked out from behind the pillar. Ms. Walker lowered the lights. Then she collected her papers and made her way out through the auditorium door.

"Why are we hiding here?" I whispered impatiently.

Zeke grinned at me. "Let's try out the trap-door," he whispered back.

"Huh?"

"Let's try it out. Quick. While there's no one in here."

I glanced quickly around the auditorium. Dark. And empty.

"Come on. Don't be a wimp," Zeke urged, pulling me toward the stage. "Let's try it out, okay? What could happen?"

I turned uncertainly to the stage. "Okay," I said.

Zeke was right. What could happen?

Zeke and I climbed onto the stage. It was darker than before. And it felt colder.

Our sneakers thudded over the floorboards. Every sound seemed to echo over the whole auditorium.

"This trapdoor is so cool!" Zeke exclaimed. "Too bad you don't get to use it in the play."

I gave him a playful shove and started to reply. But I suddenly felt one of my sneezing attacks coming on. The dusty auditorium curtain must have triggered my allergies.

I have the worst allergies in creation. I am allergic to absolutely everything. You name it. Dust, pollen, cats, dogs — even some sweaters.

When I have an allergy attack, sometimes I sneeze thirteen or fourteen times in a row. My all-time record is seventeen.

Zeke likes to count my sneezes. He thinks he's a riot. He slaps the floor and yells, "Seven! Eight! Nine!"

Ha-ha. After ten sneezes in a row, I'm in no mood for jokes. I'm usually a pitiful, dripping mess with foggy glasses.

We tiptoed over to the trapdoor. "Check the floor around there," Zeke said quietly. "Find that peg that makes it work."

Zeke stood on the trapdoor while I searched for the peg in the darkness. I desperately tried to hold in my sneezes, but it wasn't easy.

Then the small peg on the stage floor caught my eye. "Hey — I found it!" I shouted happily.

Zeke glanced nervously around the auditorium. "*Ssshhh!* Someone will hear you!"

"Sorry," I whispered. Then I realized I couldn't hold out any longer. My eyes were watering like crazy, and I just had to sneeze.

I grabbed a handful of tissues from my pocket and put the whole wad up to my nose. Then I started sneezing. I tried to keep them as silent as possible.

"Four! Five!" Zeke counted.

Luckily, it wasn't a record-breaking attack. I only made it to seven. I wiped my nose and shoved the dirty tissues in my pocket. It was gross, but I had nowhere else to throw them.

"Okay, Zeke, here goes!" I cried.

I stepped on the peg and jumped beside Zeke on the trapdoor.

We heard a clanking sound. Then a rumbling. Then a grinding.

The square section of floor began to lower itself.

Zeke grabbed my arm. "Hey — this thing is kind of shaky!" he cried.

"You're not scared — are you?" I challenged him.

"No way!" he insisted.

The clanking grew louder. The square platform shook beneath us as we slid down. Down, down — until the stage disappeared, and we were surrounded by darkness.

I expected the platform to come to a stop just beneath the stage. That's where it stopped for Ms. Walker.

But, to my surprise, the platform kept dropping.

And it picked up speed as it slid farther and farther down.

"Hey — what's happening?" Zeke cried, holding on to my arm.

"How far down does this thing go?" I wondered out loud.

"Ohh!" Zeke and I both cried out as the platform finally hit the bottom with a hard *thud*!

We were both thrown to the floor.

I scrambled to my feet quickly. "Are you okay?"

"Yeah. I guess." Zeke definitely sounded scared.

We seemed to be in a long black tunnel.

Dark. And silent.

I don't like to admit it. But I was very close to being scared, too.

Suddenly, the silence was broken by a soft, raspy noise.

I felt panic choke my throat. That sound. What was it?

The sound repeated softly, steadily.

Like breathing.

My heart pounded in my chest. Yes! Breathing. The raspy breathing of a strange creature. So close to me.

Right next to me.

Zeke!

"Zeke — why are you breathing like that?" I demanded, feeling my heartbeat slow to normal.

"Breathing like what?" he whispered.

"Oh. Never mind," I muttered. He was breathing that way because he was scared. We were both scared. But there was no way we would ever admit it to each other.

We both raised our eyes to the auditorium ceiling. It was a small square glow in the far distance. It seemed to be miles and miles above us.

Zeke turned to me. "Where do you think we are?"

"We're about a mile beneath the stage," I replied, feeling a chill.

"No kidding, Sherlock," Zeke replied nastily.

"If you're so smart, you tell *me*!" I challenged him.

"I don't think it's the basement," he said thoughtfully. "I think we're way below the basement."

"It feels like it's a big tunnel or something," I said, trying to keep my voice from shaking. "Want to explore?"

He didn't answer for a long moment. "Too dark to explore," he replied finally.

I didn't really want to explore. I was just pretending to be brave. Usually, I liked having the creeps. But being way down here was *too* creepy, even for me.

"We'll come back with flashlights," Zeke said softly.

"Yeah. Flashlights," I repeated. I didn't plan to *ever* come back!

I played nervously with the denim scrunchie on my wrist and stared out into the darkness. Something bothered me. Something didn't make sense.

"Zeke," I said thoughtfully, "why would the stage trapdoor come all the way down here?"

"I don't know. Maybe so the Phantom can get home quicker after he haunts the auditorium!" Zeke joked.

I punched him in the arm. "No jokes about the Phantom — okay?"

If there really is a phantom, I told myself, *this is where he would live.*

"Let's get out of here!" Zeke said, staring up at the square of light so far above our heads. "I'm going to be late for dinner."

"Yeah, sure," I replied, folding my arms across my chest. "Just one question, Mr. Know-It-All."

"What question?" Zeke asked uncertainly.

"How do we get back up?"

We both thought about that one for a while.

After a minute or so, I saw Zeke drop to his knees and begin running his hand along the platform floor. "There's got to be a peg to push down here," he said.

"No. The peg is up there," I replied, pointing way up to the stage floor.

"Then there's got to be a switch or a lever or a button to push!" Zeke cried. His voice grew high and shrill.

"Where? Where could it be?" My voice sounded just as shrill, just as frightened.

We both started feeling around in the darkness, feeling for something we could push, or pull, or turn. Something to make the little square platform rise up again and carry us back up to the auditorium.

But after a few minutes of desperate searching, I gave up.

"We're trapped down here, Zeke," I murmured. "We're trapped."

30

"This is all your fault," I muttered.

I don't know why I said that. I guess I was so frightened, I didn't know *what* I was saying.

Zeke forced a laugh. "Hey, I *like* it down here!" he boasted. "I may just stay down here for a while. You know. Do some exploring." He was trying to sound brave. But his voice came out tiny and trembling.

He wasn't fooling me. No way.

"How could you bring us down here?" I cried.

"You wanted to come, too!" he shot back.

"I did not!" I screamed. "Ms. Walker *told* us this thing isn't safe! And now we'll be down here all night! Maybe forever!"

"Unless we're eaten by rats!" Zeke joked.

"I'm *sick* of your stupid jokes!" I shouted. I totally lost it. I gave him a hard shove with both hands. He went sprawling off the platform.

It was so dark, I couldn't see him for a moment.

"Ow!" I cried out as he shoved me back.

31

Then I shoved him harder.

Then he shoved me harder than that.

I stumbled back — onto some kind of a switch. My back hit the switch.

A loud clanking sound made me nearly jump out of my skin.

"Brooke — jump back on! Quick!" Zeke screamed.

I leaped back onto the platform just as it started to move.

Up, up. Sliding slowly but steadily.

The square of light above our heads grew larger and brighter as we rose back up to the auditorium.

"Hey!" I cried out as the platform stopped with a jolt.

"Way to go, Brookie!" Zeke yelled happily. He slapped me on the back.

"Don't celebrate yet," I told him. We still weren't back on the stage. The platform had stopped about five feet down from the top. Just where it had been for Ms. Walker.

I guessed that the only way to raise it all the way up was to step on the peg onstage.

"Give me a boost up," Zeke urged eagerly.

I cupped my hands together. He lowered his sneaker into my hands.

"Wait!" he cried, stepping back down. "Whoa! What if the Phantom is up there waiting for us? Maybe *you* should go first!"

"Ha-ha. Very funny," I said, rolling my eyes. "Remind me to laugh later."

"Okay, okay. I'll go first," he muttered.

He put his sneaker into my cupped hands, reached up to the stage floor, and I gave him a boost.

I watched him scramble onto the stage. He disappeared from view.

I waited for him to reach down for me.

A whole minute went by.

"Zeke?" The word came out tiny and weak.

I waited some more. Listening hard.

I couldn't hear him up there. Where was he?

"Zeke? Where are you?" I called up. "Come on. Raise the platform. Or give me a hand," I called up. "I can't make it by myself.

Another minute passed. It seemed like an hour.

I suddenly realized what Zeke was trying to do.

That big jerk! He was trying to scare me!

"Hey! Enough!" I shouted.

I'd had more than enough of Zeke Matthews for one day.

"Zeke!" I yelled. "Give me a break! Get me up!"

Finally, his hands lowered down over the side.

"It's about time!" I shouted angrily.

I grabbed both hands and let him pull me up to the stage.

I shook my hair back. My eyes were slowly adjusting to the brighter light. "You know, you're not funny!" I snapped. "Keeping me waiting down there was really —"

I stopped and swallowed hard. It wasn't Zeke who had pulled me from the trapdoor.

A strange pair of dark, angry eyes stared into mine.

I swallowed hard. A strange little man stared
back at me, an angry scowl on his face. He wore
baggy gray pants and a loose-fitting gray sweat-
shirt, torn at the collar.

His thick white hair fell wild and unbrushed
over his forehead like a floor mop. He had a deep
purple scar down the side of his face, nearly as
long as the scar on Zeke's creature mask.

I could see that he was old. But he was tiny, no
bigger than a kid. He stood only an inch or two
taller than Zeke.

As he squinted at me with his strange gray
eyes, his face twisted into an ugly frown.

He looks like a phantom! The frightening
thought flashed through my mind.

"Wh-who are you?" I stammered.

"I'm Emile. The night janitor," the man
rasped.

"Where's my friend Zeke?" I demanded in a
shrill, frightened voice.

"Brooke, I'm over here," Zeke called out from behind me.

I whirled around. Zeke stood on the other side of the trapdoor. He had his hands shoved deep into his jeans pockets. He was biting his lower lip.

"Zeke!" I cried. "What's going on? Why —"

"The school is closed!" The janitor growled. He had a hoarse voice, like sandpaper. "What are you two doing in here?"

Zeke and I exchanged glances. Zeke took a step forward. "We . . . uh . . . stayed for play rehearsal," he told the man.

"That's right," I chimed in. "We had a late rehearsal."

The janitor continued to squint suspiciously at me. "Play rehearsal?" he repeated. "Then where is everybody else?"

I hesitated. This guy was scaring me so much, my legs wobbled. "We left," I blurted out. "But we had to come back to get my jacket."

Behind Emile, I saw Zeke nodding, approving my lie.

"How do you know about the trapdoor?" the janitor demanded in his sandpaper voice.

I hesitated. *It's strange that I've never seen him in the school building before*, I thought.

"Ms. Walker, our teacher, showed it to us," Zeke said softly. I could see that he was as scared as I was.

The man leaned closer to me, squinting so that one side of his face was completely twisted up. "Don't you know how *dangerous* it is?" he whispered.

He leaned even closer, so close that I could feel his hot breath on my face. His pale gray eyes stared into mine. *"Don't you know how dangerous it is?"*

Zeke and I talked on the phone that night. "That man wasn't trying to *warn* us," I told Zeke. "He was trying to *scare* us."

"Well, he didn't scare *me* at all," Zeke boasted. "I'm sorry if he got *you* upset, Brookie."

Oh, wow, I thought. *Sometimes Zeke is such a phoney.*

"If you weren't scared, how come you were shaking all the way home?" I demanded.

"I wasn't shaking. I was just exercising," Zeke joked. "You know. Working out the calf muscles."

"Give me a break," I moaned. "How come we've never seen that janitor before?"

"Because he's *not* a janitor. He is . . . *the PHANTOM!*" Zeke cried in a deep, scary voice.

I didn't laugh. "Get serious," I told him. "It wasn't a joke. He was really trying to frighten us."

"Hope you don't have nightmares, Brookie," Zeke replied, laughing.

I hung up on him.

On Tuesday morning, I walked to school with my little brother, Jeremy. As we walked, I talked about the play.

I told Jeremy the whole story. But I left out the part about the trapdoor. Ms. Walker said it would be better if we kept it a secret until the performance.

"Is it really scary?" Jeremy asked me. Jeremy is seven, and he gets scared if you say "boo" to him. Once, I made him watch the movie *Poltergeist* with me, and he woke up screaming every night for three weeks.

"Yeah, it's pretty scary," I told him. "But not scary like *Friday the 13th* scary."

Jeremy seemed relieved. He really hated scary things. On Halloween, he hid in his room! I would never make him watch *Friday the 13th.* He would probably have nightmares till he was fifty!

"The play has a surprise," I added. "And it's a pretty awesome surprise."

"What is it?" Jeremy demanded.

I reached over and messed up his hair. It's chestnut-brown, like mine. "If I told you that," I said, making a funny voice, "it wouldn't be a surprise, would it?"

"You sound just like Mom!" Jeremy cried.

What an insult!

I dropped him off at his school and then crossed the street to my school. As I made my way down the hall, I thought about my part in the play. Esmerelda had so many lines. I wondered if I could memorize them all in time.

And I wondered if my old stage fright would come back. Last year, I had terrible stage fright in *Guys and Dolls*. And I didn't even have any lines to say!

I walked into the classroom, said good morning to some kids, made my way to my table — and stopped.

"Hey!" A boy I had never seen before was at my place.

He was kind of cute. He had dark brown hair and bright green eyes. He was wearing a big red-and-black flannel shirt over black sweatpants.

He had made himself right at home. His books and notebooks were spread out. And he was tilting back in my chair with his black high-tops resting on the table.

"You're in my place," I said, standing over him.

He gazed up at me with those green eyes. "No, I'm not," he replied casually. "This is *my* place."

"Excuse me?" I said, staring down at him.

He blushed. "I *think* this is where Ms. Walker told me to sit." He glanced around nervously.

I saw an empty spot at the table behind mine. "She probably meant over there," I said, pointing. "I've been in this seat all year. Next to Zeke." I motioned to Zeke's chair. Zeke wasn't there. He was late, as usual.

The boy blushed even darker. "Sorry," he muttered shyly. "I hate being the new kid." He started to gather his books together.

"This is your first day?" I asked. I introduced myself.

"I'm Brian Colson," he replied, climbing to his feet. "My family just moved to Woods Mill. From Indiana."

I said I'd never been to Indiana. It was a boring thing to say, but it was true.

"You're Brooke Rodgers?" he asked, studying me. "I heard you got the starring role. In the play."

"How did you hear that already?" I demanded.

"Some kids were talking about it on the bus. You must be a good actress, huh?" he added shyly.

"I guess. I don't know. Sometimes I get pretty bad stage fright," I told him.

I don't know why I told him that. Sometimes I just rattle on. I guess that's why my parents call me Babbling Brooke.

Brian smiled and sighed. "Back at my school in Indiana, I was in all the plays," he told me. "But I never had the lead role. I wish I had moved here sooner. Then I could have tried out for *The Phantom.*"

I tried to picture Brian onstage in a play, but I couldn't. He didn't seem like the acting type to me. He seemed so shy. And he kept blushing all the time.

But I decided to give the poor guy a break. "Brian, why don't you come to rehearsal with me this afternoon?" I suggested. "Maybe you can get a small part or something."

Brian smiled as if I'd just offered him a million dollars. "You mean it?" he asked, wide-eyed.

"Sure," I replied. "No big deal."

Zeke came slinking into his seat, his eyes on Ms. Walker's desk. "Am I late?" he whispered.

I shook my head. Then I started to introduce him to Brian. But Ms. Walker stepped into the room and closed the door. Time for class to begin.

Brian hurried to his place at the other table. I started to sit down but realized I'd left my science notebook in my locker.

"Be right back!" I called to Ms. Walker. I hurried out the door and jogged around the corner to my locker.

"Hey!" To my surprise, the locker door stood open.

That's weird, I thought. I remembered locking it.

I pulled the door open the rest of the way. Started to reach inside for my notebook.

And let out a startled gasp.

Someone was in there — and he was staring right at me!

His ugly blue-and-green face grinned out at me.

I gasped again and clamped my hand over my mouth. Then I cracked up laughing.

Zeke and his dumb rubber-creature mask.

"Well, you got me this time, Zeke!" I murmured out loud.

Then I saw the folded-up sheet of paper dangling beneath the mask. Some kind of note?

I pulled it out and unfolded it. Scribbled in red crayon was a message:

STAY AWAY FROM MY
HOME SWEET HOME

"Ha-ha," I murmured. "Very good, Zeke. Very amusing."

I pulled out my science notebook, slammed the locker shut, and locked it. Then I hurried back to the classroom.

Ms. Walker stood behind her desk. She had just finished introducing Brian to everyone. Now she was reading the morning announcements. I slid into my seat beside Zeke. "You didn't scare me one bit," I lied.

He looked up from his math notebook. Zeke always did his math homework first thing in class. "Huh?" He flashed me his innocent look.

"Your mask," I whispered. "It didn't scare me."

"Mask? What mask?" he replied, tapping the pencil eraser against my arm.

I shoved him away. "Stop acting stupid," I said sharply. "Your note wasn't funny, either. You can do better than that."

"I didn't write you any note, Brooke," Zeke replied impatiently. "I don't know what you're talking about. Really."

"For sure," I said rolling my eyes. "You don't know anything about the mask in my locker or the note, right?"

"Shut up and let me finish my math," he said, staring down at his textbook. "You're not making any sense."

"Oh. Well. I guess the *real* Phantom did it, then," I said.

He ignored me. He was scribbling equations in his notebook.

What a phoney baloney! I thought. *Zeke did it, and he knows it.*

For sure.

44

*   *   *

After school, I led Brian to the auditorium. I practically had to drag him up on the stage. He was so shy!

"Ms. Walker, are there any parts still available?" I asked. "Brian is really interested in being in the play."

Ms. Walker glanced up from the script in her hands. I saw that she had scribbled notes all over the script. She studied Brian.

"I'm really sorry, Brian," she said, shaking her head. "You came to school a few days too late."

Brian blushed. I've never seen anyone blush so often.

"There aren't any speaking parts left," Ms. Walker told him. "They've all been given out."

"Do you need a stand-in for anyone?" Brian asked. "I'm a very fast memorizer. I could memorize more than one part."

Wow, I thought. *He really is eager to be in the play.*

"Well, we really don't need any more stand-ins," Ms. Walker told him. "But, I have an idea. You can join the scenery crew if you wish."

"Great!" Brian exclaimed with real enthusiasm.

"Go see Tina over there," Ms. Walker told him, pointing to the group of kids meeting at the back wall of the stage. Tina was busily pointing out where she wanted the scenery to go, motioning

45

dramatically with both hands, making everyone follow her all around the stage.

Brian seemed really happy. I watched him trot over to find Tina.

I took a seat in the auditorium and concentrated on my script. I was in practically every scene. How could I possibly memorize my whole part? I sighed and slouched back, slinging my feet over the seat in front of me.

I was memorizing my third line in the play, which went, *"What proof do you have that this man might be dangerous?"* when all the lights suddenly went out.

A total blackout! I couldn't see a thing.

Kids started to shout. "Hey! Who turned out the lights?"

"I can't see!"

"What's happening? Turn them back on!"

I sat straight up when I heard the shrill scream.

A terrifying scream — like an animal howl — that ripped through the darkness and exploded over the auditorium.

"No! Noooo!" I heard Corey Sklar moan.

And then I heard someone else cry out, "It's coming from up on the catwalk!"

Another shrill wail rose up over the frightened cries of my friends.

"Turn on the lights!" I heard Corey plead. "Please — turn on the lights!"

46

Other frightened voices called out, "Who is screaming?"

"Somebody — do something!"

"There's someone up on the catwalk!"

The auditorium lights flickered back on.

Another long howl from above the stage forced me to raise my eyes.

And I saw him. A blue-and-green-masked creature wearing a shiny black cape.

Gripping a long, heavy rope, he came swinging down from high on the catwalk.

As he swung down to the stage, he threw his head back and laughed a horrifying evil laugh.

I jumped to my feet and stared in amazement.

The Phantom!

The Phantom landed hard on his feet. His shoes hit the stage floor with a *thud.*

He let go of the rope and it flew away from him.

The blue-and-green face glanced quickly around the stage. Tina and her scenery crew stood frozen against the wall, staring at him in horrified silence. Ms. Walker appeared stunned. She had her arms tightly crossed over her chest.

The Phantom's cape swirled around him as he stomped one shoe on the stage.

He's short, I realized, standing and staring from down in the second row of seats. He's about Zeke's height. Maybe an inch or two taller.

Or maybe he's *exactly* Zeke's height — because he *is* Zeke!

"Zeke! Hey — Zeke!" I called.

The ugly masked face peered out to the auditorium. The Phantom started to sink. His feet disappeared. The legs of his dark pants. Down. Down.

He had stepped on the peg and was riding the trapdoor down.

"Zeke!" I yelled. I ran up the aisle and pulled myself up onto the stage. "Zeke — you're not funny!" I shouted.

But the Phantom had vanished below the stage.

I ran up to the opening in the stage and stared down into the darkness. Ms. Walker stepped up beside me, an angry scowl on her face. "Was that Zeke?" she asked me. "Was that really Zeke?"

"I — I'm not sure," I stammered. "I think so."

"Zeke!" Ms. Walker called down into the opening. "Zeke — are you down there?"

No reply.

The platform had lowered all the way down. I couldn't see anything but a deep well of blackness.

Kids gathered around the opening, chattering excitedly, laughing and teasing each other. "Was that Zeke?" I heard Corey ask. "Was Zeke wearing that dumb mask again?"

"Is Zeke going to ruin our rehearsal today?" Ms. Walker demanded angrily. "Does he think we *need* to be scared every afternoon?"

I shrugged. I couldn't answer.

"Maybe it wasn't Zeke," I heard Corey say. He sounded very frightened.

"It had to be Zeke. Zeke — are you there?" Ms. Walker shouted, cupping her hands around her mouth. She turned slowly, her eyes darting over the stage and then all the seats of the auditorium. "Zeke Matthews? Can you hear me?"

No answer. No sign of Zeke.

"He's *your* friend, Brooke," Tina said nastily. "Don't you know where he is? Can't you tell him to stop ruining our play?"

I sputtered an answer. I was so angry, I didn't know what I was saying.

I mean, Zeke is my friend. But I'm not *responsible* for him!

Tina was just trying to make me look bad and score some points with Ms. Walker.

"Okay, scenery people," Ms. Walker instructed. "Back to work. I'll take care of this. The rest of you —"

She stopped. We all heard it. The loud clanking sound.

A loud hum rose up over the clanking.

"The trapdoor — it's coming back up!" I cried, pointing.

"Good," Ms. Walker said, crossing her arms over her chest again. She narrowed her eyes at the opening in the stage floor. "Now I will let Zeke know how we feel about his little joke. His *last* little joke, if I have anything to say about it!"

Uh-oh, I thought. *Poor Zeke.*

Ms. Walker was a really good teacher, and a really nice person, too — until you got on her bad side. But once you did that, once you made her angry, once you had her crossing her arms and squinting her eyes at you — then you were in major trouble.

Because she could be really mean.

I knew that Zeke was just having some fun. He loved being the center of attention. And he loved to scare people. He especially loved to scare *me*.

This was a game for him, I knew. He was trying to show everyone that they were scaredy-cat wimps, and he wasn't.

Zeke played this game all the time.

But this time it had backfired. This time he had gone too far.

And Ms. Walker was waiting for him, arms crossed, eyes squinting.

Will she toss him out of the play? I wondered. *Or will she just yell at him until his ears curl?*

The hum grew louder. The stage floor vibrated.

We all heard the platform stop — its usual five feet below the stage.

Poor Zeke, I thought. *He's standing there innocently. He doesn't know what he's in for.*

Poor Zeke.

I peered down into the opening — and gasped.

The platform was empty. No one there.

Zeke — or whoever it was — had sent it back up empty. And had disappeared into the dark tunnels far below the school.

Zeke wouldn't do that, I told myself. *Even Zeke wouldn't be crazy enough to go down in the darkness by himself. Without a flashlight. Without a clue as to what was down there.*

Would he?

Yes, he would. I answered my own question. *If he thought he could* really *terrify us, Zeke would do anything!*

Ms. Walker canceled the rehearsal. She told the scenery crew to stay and paint the backdrop. She told the rest of us to go home and study our parts.

"I'm going to have a long talk with Zeke when I find him," she muttered. Then she turned and made her way quickly out of the auditorium.

I took my time walking home. I thought about Zeke all the way. I was thinking so hard, I walked right past my house!

Down the block, I saw Zeke's mother's red Pontiac pull up their driveway. Shielding my eyes against the late afternoon sun, I saw Mrs. Matthews climb out of the car. And then I saw Zeke on the other side.

"Hey! Zeke!" I shouted as I went running across the lawns toward him. "Zeke!"

His mother waved to me and disappeared into the house. Zeke looked surprised to see me. "Is play rehearsal over so early?" he asked.

"Yes. Thanks to you," I muttered.

"Huh?" He gave me his innocent look again. "What did *I* do?"

"You didn't scare me, Zeke," I told him. "No one thought it was funny. And now you're in a load of trouble with Ms. Walker."

He narrowed his eyes and scrunched up his face, pretending not to understand. "What are you talking about, Brooke? How can I be in trouble? I wasn't even there!"

"You were there long enough," I told him.

He shook his head. His freckles seemed to grow darker. His blond hair fluttered in the wind. "No, I wasn't," he said quietly. "I *told* Ms. Walker I wouldn't be there. I told her this morning that I had to miss rehearsal."

"So you could get into your mask and cape and come flying down from the catwalk?" I asked suspiciously.

"No. I told her I had a dentist appointment."

I gaped at him in shock. My mouth dropped open.

"What's your problem, Brooke?" he demanded. "It was only a checkup."

"You — you really weren't at school?" I stammered.

He shook his head. "No way."

"Then who was the Phantom?" I asked in a tiny voice.

A strange smile spread over Zeke's face.

"It *was* you!" I cried angrily. "You did your Phantom act, and *then* you went to your dentist appointment! *Didn't* you, Zeke! *Didn't* you!"

He only laughed. He wouldn't answer.

After school the next afternoon, I walked with Brian to the auditorium. He looked cute in a black vest over a plain white T-shirt and faded jeans. "How are you doing with Tina?" I asked.

"Okay, I guess," Brian replied. "She's a little bossy. But she's letting me design the backdrop pretty much on my own."

I waved to some kids who were heading out the door for home. We turned the corner. I saw Corey and Tina walking into the auditorium.

"Did Zeke work things out with Ms. Walker?" Brian asked. "I saw him talking to her this morning."

"I guess," I replied. "She's letting Zeke stay in the play — for now."

"Do you think it was Zeke who pulled that stunt yesterday?" Brian asked.

I nodded. "Yes, I do. Zeke likes scaring people. He's been doing it since we were little. I think Zeke is trying to scare us. He's trying to make us think there's a real Phantom in the school." I smiled at Brian. "But I don't scare so easy!" I declared.

Soon after rehearsal started, Ms. Walker called Zeke and me onstage. She said she wanted to walk us through one of our scenes together. She wanted to show us where we should stand when we said our lines. She called it "blocking."

She also asked Tina Powell and Robert Hernandez, Zeke's understudy, to come up onstage. Ms. Walker said they should know all the blocking, too. Just in case.

Just in case? I thought. Then I remembered Tina's warning: "*So if you get sick or something and you can't be in the show, I'll play the part of Esmerelda.*"

"Well, Tina, I hate to disappoint you," I muttered to myself, "but I plan to be perfectly fine. So have fun painting your scenery. It's the only time you'll be onstage."

I know, I know. That's kind of mean. But Tina deserved it.

Ms. Walker showed Zeke where to stand. I stood off to the side of the stage with Tina, waiting for my cue.

"I guess Ms. Walker and Zeke worked things out," Tina said. "I heard him this morning telling her he was at the dentist's, and so he couldn't be the one to swing down from the ceiling."

I started to tell Tina to be quiet so I could hear my cue. But I was too late. I already heard Ms. Walker calling my name.

"Brooke Rodgers!" She sounded angry. "What's going on over there? You're supposed to be onstage!"

"Thanks a bunch, Tina," I muttered under my breath. I ran out onto the stage. Glancing back, I could see Tina laughing to herself.

I couldn't believe it! Tina had made me miss my cue on purpose!

Onstage, I didn't know where I was supposed to stand. I didn't even know what page of the script we were on.

What was my next line?

I couldn't remember.

In a panic, I stared out at the kids in the auditorium seats. They all stared back at me, waiting for me to speak.

I opened my mouth, but nothing came out.

"The line is, *'Is somebody down here?'*" Tina yelled loudly from offstage.

Oh, wow, I thought unhappily. *Tina will do anything to show me up! She's just hoping Ms. Walker will kick me out of the play.*

I felt so angry, my head was spinning. I couldn't think straight. I repeated the line, then took a deep breath to calm down.

Zeke had the next line. He was supposed to appear onstage and scare Esmerelda.

But Zeke wasn't onstage. He wasn't anywhere in sight!

I peered out into the auditorium. Ms. Walker stood at the foot of the stage. She had her hands on her waist. She tapped one toe impatiently on the hard floor.

The auditorium grew silent, except for that tap. *Tap, tap, tap, tap, tap.* Ms. Walker seemed to be *very* annoyed.

"Where is Zeke?" she asked wearily. "What is he doing now? Is he going to come flying down from the catwalk in full costume or something?"

I should have guessed what Zeke was up to. But it didn't dawn on me until I heard the familiar noise. The loud clanking. Followed by the hum.

The trapdoor platform! It was rising!

I sighed. "Here comes Zeke," I told Ms. Walker.

And a second later, Zeke's blue-and-green-masked head appeared.

I stepped back and watched him rise from down below. It looked awesome. Really dramatic.

Slowly, he appeared, rising up over the stage floor.

He reached the top and just stood there for a long moment, staring out at the auditorium, as if posing for a picture. He was in full costume: his mask, a black cape down to his ankles, black shirt and pants.

What a ham! I thought. *He really loves having everyone stare at him and think he's hot stuff!*

And then he stepped toward me, taking quick strides. Through the mask, he raised his eyes to me.

I tried to remember what I was supposed to say next.

But before I could utter a sound, he grabbed both of my shoulders. He shook them really hard. Too hard.

Ease up, Zeke, I thought. *It's only rehearsal.*

"Go away!" he cried in a furious whisper.

I remembered what I was supposed to say. I opened my mouth to speak . . .

But then I froze.

I saw someone waving to me from the edge of the stage.

Waving frantically.

It was Zeke!

13

I knew I was in major trouble.

If Zeke was standing way over there, who was shaking my shoulders, grinning at me through the ugly mask?

"*Help! Somebody — help me!*" I screamed, struggling to free myself.

"No, Brooke!" Ms. Walker called out to me. "The line is, '*Help! Help me, Father!*'"

She didn't get it.

Couldn't she see that there was a *real* phantom up here trying to shake me to death?

Suddenly, the Phantom lowered his masked face and whispered harshly in my ear, "*Stay away. Stay away from my home sweet home!*"

I gazed into his eyes.

They looked familiar to me.

Who was he? I knew I'd seen him before.

But before I could remember, he spun away from me, took a diving leap off the stage, and ran up the long aisle, his cape flowing behind him.

I stood watching in horror as he disappeared out through the auditorium doors.

Some kids laughed. I heard Tina mutter to someone, "Was that in the script?"

Zeke came running over to me. "Brookie, are you all right?"

"I — I don't know," I replied. I felt really shaken up.

"That was *weird*!" Zeke exclaimed.

Ms. Walker came striding across the stage, swinging her clipboard in one hand. She had a very confused expression on her face. "Can anyone explain what just happened here?" she asked.

"There's a real phantom in this school," Zeke said softly. He narrowed his eyes at me thoughtfully.

We were sitting in the front row of the auditorium. Brian scraped at a smudge of black paint on the back of his hand. I sat between the two boys, studying Zeke.

The lights had been dimmed. Rehearsal had ended a few minutes before. I could hear a few voices out in the hall. The door had just closed behind Ms. Walker.

"Why are you staring at me like that?" Zeke demanded.

"I'm still wondering if you aren't responsible for *everything*," I told him bluntly.

He rolled his eyes. "Yeah. Sure," he muttered. "How could I be in two places at once today, Brooke? Answer me that. That's pretty tricky, even for someone as brilliant and clever as me!"

I laughed. "It's possible," I replied.

"I can't get this paint off," Brian moaned. "Look. I got it on my shirt, too."

"Is it washable paint?" Zeke asked.

"How should I know?" Brian replied unhappily. "I didn't read the label on the can. Do you read labels on cans?"

"Zeke only reads cereal boxes," I joked.

"Will you stop kidding around?" Zeke demanded impatiently. "We've got a real phantom in this school. And for some reason, he's trying to mess up our play."

I was still studying Zeke's face, trying to figure out if he was telling the truth. "I saw you talking to Andy Seltzer this morning before school," I told Zeke. "You could have planned this whole phantom thing with him. You gave Andy the costume, right? You told him what to do. You and Andy planned the whole thing. Right?"

Zeke's mouth dropped open. "Huh? Why would I do that?"

"To scare me," I replied. "To scare everyone. To make us think there's a real phantom. And then when you get us really scared, you laugh and say *'Gotcha!'* And we all feel like total jerks."

A smile crossed Zeke's face. "Wish I'd thought of that," he murmured. "But I'm serious, Brooke. I know you don't believe me, but I didn't plan anything with Andy. And I didn't —"

Tina hopped down from the stage. I guessed she'd been working on scenery behind the curtain. "Are you feeling better, Brooke?" she asked coldly.

I turned to her. "Feeling better? I'm okay. What do you mean?"

"You looked so stressed out onstage, I thought maybe you were sick," Tina replied nastily. "Are you coming down with the flu? I hear there's a really bad one going around."

"I'm fine," I said curtly.

"Is this paint washable?" Brian asked Tina.

Tina shrugged. "Beats me. Try turpentine." She smiled at Brian. "You're doing a good job on the backdrop." Then she turned back to me and her smile faded. "At least *someone* is doing a good job on this play."

Before I could reply, she turned and hurried across the aisle and out the auditorium door.

"She's *praying* I get the flu," I told Zeke. "Isn't that sick?"

He didn't reply. He was thinking so hard about the Phantom, I don't think he even heard me.

"Do you think Tina could be doing all these terrible things?" I asked. "Just to frighten me away so that she can be Esmerelda?"

"That's crazy," Zeke replied softly.

"Yeah. I guess," I agreed.

Brian just kept trying to peel the black paint off his hand.

"Let's go home," I suggested. "It's really late. Maybe we can talk about the Phantom later." I climbed to my feet.

Zeke glared up at me. "You still don't believe me — do you!" he accused. "You still think this is all some plot just to scare you."

"Maybe. Maybe not," I said, climbing over him to get to the aisle. I really didn't know what to think.

Brian got up and followed me to the door. I turned back to Zeke, who was still in his seat. "Are you coming? Are you going to walk with us?"

Zeke stood up without replying. "Yeah. I guess."

We were heading down the hall to our lockers when Zeke suddenly stopped. "Oh. I forgot," he uttered.

"Forgot what?" I asked. It was nearly dinnertime. I was eager to get home. My mom was probably wondering if I'd been run over by a bus or something. Mom always imagines me run over by a bus. I don't really know why. I never knew *anyone* who was ever run over by a bus!

"My math book," Zeke said. "I have to go to the office. I left it in the auditorium the other night. I've got to see if anyone turned it in."

"I'll see you later," Brian said, backing down the hall.

"Where do you live?" I called to him.

He pointed in a direction. South, I think. "See you tomorrow!" He turned and jogged around the corner.

I followed Zeke to Mr. Levy's office. All the lights were on, but the office was empty, except for Dot, the secretary. She was shutting down her computer, getting ready to go home.

"Did anyone turn in my math book?" Zeke asked her, leaning on the counter.

"Math book?" She squinted back at Zeke thoughtfully.

"I left it in the auditorium the other night," Zeke said. "I thought maybe that guy Emile turned it in."

Dot's expression turned to confusion. "Who? Who is Emile?"

"You know," Zeke replied. "The little old guy with the white hair. The night janitor."

Dot shook her head. "You're a little mixed up, Zeke," she said. "There's no one named Emile who works at the school. We don't *have* a night janitor."

Tina Powell called me at home that night. "Just wanted to see how you're feeling," she said. "You looked so pale, Brooke."

"I'm *not* getting the flu!" I shouted. I really lost my cool. But I couldn't help it.

"I heard you sneezing a lot yesterday," Tina said, pretending to be concerned.

"I always sneeze a lot," I replied. "Bye, Tina."

"Who was that other phantom who jumped onstage this afternoon?" Tina asked before I could hang up.

"I don't know," I said. "I really —"

"That was kind of scary," Tina interrupted. "I hope you weren't *too* scared or anything, Brooke."

"See you tomorrow, Tina," I said coldly.

I hung up the phone before she could say anything else. Tina was really becoming a pain, I decided.

How much does she want to play Esmerelda?
I found myself wondering.

Just how much does she want the part? Enough to try to scare me away?

Zeke called later and convinced me that Emile *had* to be our phantom. "He lied to us, right?" Zeke asked excitedly. "He told us he worked for the school. And he tried to frighten us. It's *got* to be him," Zeke insisted.

"Yeah. Probably," I replied, twirling the scrunchie on my wrist.

"He's the right size," Zeke continued. "And he knew about the trapdoor." Zeke took a breath. "And why was he there, Brookie? Why was he there in the auditorium at night?"

"Because he's the Phantom?" I asked.

It made sense.

I agreed to get to school early so that Zeke and I could tell Ms. Walker about Emile.

That night I dreamed about the play. I was onstage in my costume. The spotlights were all on me. I stared out at the seats filled with people.

The auditorium grew silent. Everyone was waiting for Esmerelda to speak.

I opened my mouth — and realized I didn't remember what I was supposed to say.

I stared out at the faces of the audience.

I had forgotten everything. Every word. Every line.

The words had all flown away, like birds leaving a nest.

My nest was empty. My mind was a total blank.

I stood there in panic. I couldn't move. I couldn't speak.

I woke up in a cold sweat. My entire body trembled. My muscles had all knotted up. I had kicked all the covers onto the floor.

What a horrible dream.

I couldn't wait to get dressed and get to school. I wanted to forget about that awful nightmare as quickly as I could.

I had to walk Jeremy to school. So I didn't get there as early as I wanted.

Jeremy kept asking me about the play. He wanted to hear more about the Phantom. But I really didn't feel like talking about it. I kept remembering my dream, remembering the panic of standing in front of three hundred people and looking like a total jerk.

I dropped Jeremy off, then hurried across the street. I found Zeke waiting for me by the front door. He was staring impatiently at his watch.

I don't know why. It doesn't have the correct time on it. It's one of those digital watches with seventeen different controls on it. Zeke can't figure out how to set it. He can play games on it — and play a dozen different songs. But he can't get it to tell the time.

"Sorry I'm late," I said.

He grabbed my arm and pulled me right into the classroom. He wouldn't even let me get my books from my locker or take off my coat.

We marched up to Ms. Walker, who was sitting behind her desk, glancing over the morning announcements. She smiled at us, but her smile faded as she saw the solemn looks on our faces.

"Is something wrong?" Ms. Walker asked.

"Could we speak to you?" Zeke whispered, glancing at the kids already in class. "In private?"

Ms. Walker gazed up at the wall clock. "Can't it wait? The bell is going to ring in two minutes."

"It will only take a minute," Zeke promised.

She followed us out into the hall and leaned her back against the tile wall. "What's the problem?"

"There's a phantom in the school," Zeke told her breathlessly. "A real one. Brooke and I have seen him."

"Whoa!" Ms. Walker murmured, raising both hands to say *stop*.

"No! Really!" I insisted. "We *did* see him, Ms. Walker. In the auditorium. We sneaked in. To use the trapdoor, and —"

"You did *what*?" she cried, narrowing her eyes first at me, then at Zeke.

"I know, I know," Zeke said, blushing. "We weren't supposed to. But that's not the point."

"There's a phantom," I said. "And he's trying to stop the play."

"I know you think I've been doing all those things," Zeke added. "But I haven't. It's the Phantom. He —"

Ms. Walker raised her hands again. She started to say something, but the bell rang — right over our heads.

We raised our hands to protect our ears.

When the bell finally stopped clanging, Ms. Walker took a few steps toward the classroom door. It was really noisy inside. The kids were all taking advantage of her not being in there.

"I'm sorry I upset you with that story," she told us.

"Huh?" Zeke and I both cried out.

"I never should have told that old phantom story," Ms. Walker said fretfully. "It got a lot of kids upset. I apologize for scaring you."

"But you didn't!" Zeke protested. "We saw a guy, and —"

"Have you been having nightmares about a phantom?" Ms. Walker demanded.

She didn't believe us. She didn't believe a word we had said.

"Listen —" I started.

All three of us jumped when we heard a loud crash inside the room. A crash followed by wild laughter.

"Let's get inside," Ms. Walker said. She pointed at Zeke. "No more practical jokes — okay? No more jokes. We want the play to be good, don't we?"

Before we could answer, she turned and hurried into the room.

"What am I doing here?" Brian moaned. He shivered and stared up at the dark trees. "Why am I doing this?"

"You came with us because you're a nice guy," I told him, patting the shoulder of his sweater.

"No. Because I'm an *idiot*!" Brian corrected me.

This was all Zeke's idea. He came to my house after dinner. I told my parents we had our play rehearsal. A lie.

Then Zeke and I walked to school. We met Brian on the front walk, where he'd promised to wait for us.

"I can't believe Ms. Walker didn't believe us," Zeke fretted.

"Would *you* believe such a nutty story?" I demanded.

"Well, we're going to find the Phantom and prove we're right," Zeke said firmly. "We have no choice now. I mean, if Ms. Walker won't help us, we'll have to find him on our own."

"You just like a good adventure," I teased him.

He raised his eyes to mine. "Well, Brookie, if you're too scared . . ."

"But what am *I* doing here?" Brian repeated, staring at the dark school building.

"We need all the help we can get!" I told him. I gave Zeke a shove. "Let's go. I'll show you who's scared and who isn't."

"I think I'm a little scared," Brian admitted. "What if we get caught?"

"Who's going to catch us?" Zeke asked him. "There's no night janitor."

"But what if there's an alarm or something?" Brian demanded. "You know. A burglar alarm."

"For sure," I replied, rolling my eyes. "Our school can't even afford pencil sharpeners! No way they've got burglar alarms."

"Well, we're going to have to break in," Zeke said quietly, his eyes on the street. A station wagon rolled by without slowing. He tugged at the front doors. "They're locked tight."

"Maybe a side door?" Brian suggested.

We crept around to the side of the building. The playground stretched out, silent and empty. The grass glowed all silvery under the bright half-moon.

The side doors were locked, too.

And the back door that led into the band room was also locked.

I raised my eyes to the roof. The building hovered over us like some kind of dark creature. The windows reflected the white moonlight. It was the only light I could see.

"Hey — that window is open!" Zeke whispered.

We ran full speed up to the half-open window in a ground-floor classroom. It was the home ec room, I saw. Mrs. Lamston probably left the window open to let out the horrible smell of the muffins we baked that afternoon.

Zeke raised both hands to the window ledge and hoisted himself up. Sitting on the ledge, he pushed the window open wider.

A few seconds later, Brian and I followed him into the home ec room. The aroma of burned cranberry muffins lingered in the air. We tiptoed through the darkness to the door.

"Ouch!" I cried out as I banged my thigh into a low table.

"Be quiet!" Zeke scolded.

"Hey — I didn't do it on purpose!" I whispered back angrily.

He was already out the door. Brian and I followed, moving slowly, carefully.

The hall was even darker than the classroom. We kept pressed against the wall as we made our way toward the auditorium.

My heart was racing. I felt all tingly. My shoes scraped loudly over the hard floor.

Nothing to be afraid of, I told myself. *It's just the school building, the building you've been in a million times. And there's no one else here.*

Just you. Zeke. Brian. And a phantom.

A phantom who doesn't want to be found.

"I don't think I like this," Brian whispered as we edged our way around a corner. "I'm really pretty scared."

"Just pretend you're in a scary movie," I told him. "Pretend it's just a movie."

"But I don't *like* scary movies!" he protested.

"*Ssshhh*," Zeke warned. He stopped suddenly. I bumped right into him. "Try not to be a klutz, Brookie," he whispered.

"Try not to be a jerk, Zekey," I replied nastily.

I squinted into the darkness. We had reached the auditorium.

Zeke pulled open the nearest door. We peered inside. Total blackness. The air in the auditorium felt cooler.

Cool and damp.

That's because a ghost *lives in here*, I thought.

That made my heart pump even harder. I wished I could control my thoughts a little better.

Zeke fumbled with his hand against the wall and clicked on a row of lights over the section of seats to our left. The stage came into view. Empty and silent. Someone had left a ladder leaning against one wall. Several paint cans were lined up beside the ladder.

"How about turning on all the lights?" Brian suggested. He sounded really frightened.

"No way," Zeke replied, his eyes on the stage. "We want to take the Phantom by surprise, don't we? We don't want to warn him that we're coming."

Huddled close together, we made our way slowly down the center aisle toward the stage. In the dim light, long shadows fell over the seats.

Ghostly shadows, I thought.

Did a shadow move near the stage?

No.

Stop it, Brooke, I scolded myself. *Don't let your imagination go wild. Not tonight.*

I kept moving my eyes back and forth, checking out the stage and the rows of seats as we slowly made our way to the front.

Where is he? I wondered. *Where is the Phantom?*

Does he live in that dark chamber so far below the stage?

We were just a few feet from the stage when we heard the sound.

A footstep? A floorboard creaking?

All three of us stopped. All three of us heard it.

I grabbed Zeke's arm. I saw Brian's green eyes go wide with fright.

And then we heard another sound. A cough.

"We're . . . n-not alone!" I stammered.

"Wh-who's there?" I called. But my voice caught in my throat.

"Is anybody up there?" Zeke called to the stage.

No reply.

Another footstep.

Brian took a step back. He grabbed the back of a seat and held on.

"He's back there," Zeke said, leaning close to me, his eyes excited. "I know he's back there."

"Where?" I demanded, choking out the word. It was hard to talk with my heart in my throat.

I stared up at the stage. I couldn't see anyone.

I jumped when I heard another cough.

And then a clanking sound rose up over the stage and echoed through the auditorium.

At first I thought the trapdoor was about to move.

Was someone riding up on it? Was the Phantom about to rise in front of our eyes?

No.

I cried out when I saw the backdrop begin to unfurl.

The clanking sound grew louder. The backdrop was slowly being lowered at the back of the stage.

"Who is doing it?" I whispered. "Who on earth is sending it down?"

Zeke and Brian stared straight ahead and didn't reply.

Zeke's mouth was wide open. His eyes didn't blink.

Brian gripped the back of the chair with both hands.

The painted backdrop clanked down, unrolling as it lowered.

All three of us gasped as we saw what had been done to it.

It had been a gray brick theater wall. Brian and several other kids had worked for days on it, sketching it out, then painting it brick by brick.

"Who — who *did* that to my painting?" Brian cried out.

Zeke and I remained staring at it in silent horror.

The gray wall had been covered with red paint splotches and thick red smears.

It looked as if someone had dipped a wide brush in red paint, then smeared and stabbed it all over the backdrop.

"It's ruined!" Brian declared shrilly.

Zeke was the first to move. He raised his hands to the stage floor and pulled himself up onto the stage. Brian and I followed after him.

"Who's here?" Zeke called out, cupping his hands around his mouth. "Who's in here?"

Silence.

Someone is here, I knew. *Someone* had to lower that backdrop so that we could see what had been done to it.

"Who's here? Where are you?" Zeke repeated.

Again, no reply.

We moved closer, making our way slowly, keeping close together.

And as we stepped up to it, words came into view. They were scrawled across the bottom, thick letters in heavy red paint.

I stopped and squinted to read the message in the dim light:

STAY AWAY FROM MY HOME SWEET HOME

"Whoa," I murmured. I felt a chill roll down my back.

Then I heard a side door being pulled open.

All three of us turned away from the backdrop in time to see a figure step into the auditorium.

We cried out in surprise when we saw who it was.

She stood gaping up at us. She blinked her eyes several times, as if she didn't believe what she was seeing.

"I — I am really shocked," Ms. Walker said finally.

I swallowed hard. I struggled to say something, but no sound would come out.

Zeke and Brian stood frozen like me.

"I am so disappointed in all three of you," Ms. Walker said, stepping closer. "Breaking and entering is a serious crime. And the three of you have no business —"

She stopped short and let out a little gurgle as her eyes fell on the backdrop. She had been so surprised to find Zeke, Brian, and me onstage, she hadn't seen it — until now.

"Oh, no! Oh, good heavens!" she cried, raising both hands to her face. She tilted. Sort of toppled from side to side. I thought she was about to fall over!

"How *could* you?" she gasped. She hurried across the stage, her eyes on the paint-splotched backdrop. "How could you ruin it? All the students worked for so many days to get it right. How could you ruin it for everyone?"

"We didn't," Zeke said quietly.

"We didn't do it," I repeated.

She shook her head hard, as if trying to shake us away. "I'm afraid I've caught you red-handed," she said quietly, almost sadly. I saw tears brim in her eyes.

"Ms. Walker, really —" I started.

She raised a hand to stop me. "Was it so important to you three to have your little joke?" she asked, her voice trembling.

"Ms. Walker —"

"Was it so important to make everyone believe there is a phantom? So important that you broke into the school — committed a serious crime — and then completely destroyed the scenery for our play? Was your joke so important?"

"We really didn't do it," I insisted, my voice trembling, too.

Ms. Walker stepped forward and rubbed a finger over a red paint splotch on the backdrop. When she pulled the finger away, it was smeared with red paint.

"The paint is still wet," she said, her eyes burning accusingly into mine. "There's no one else here. Are you going to keep lying to me all night?"

"If you'd just give us a chance —" Zeke started.

"I'm especially disappointed in you, Brian," Ms. Walker said, shaking her head, a frown tightening her features. "You just started at this school a week or so ago. You should be on your best behavior."

Brian blushed redder than I've ever seen a human blush. He lowered his eyes, as if he were guilty.

I took a deep breath. "Ms. Walker, you *have* to let us explain!" I cried shrilly. "We really didn't do this! We found it like this! Really!"

Ms. Walker opened her mouth to speak, but changed her mind. "Okay." She crossed her arms over her skinny chest. "Go ahead. But I want the *truth.*"

"The truth," I said. I raised my right hand, as if swearing an oath. "Brian, Zeke, and I *did* sneak into the school. We didn't really break in. We climbed in through a window."

"Why?" Ms. Walker demanded sternly. "What are you doing here? Why aren't you home where you should be?"

"We came to look for the Phantom," Zeke broke in. He swept his blond hair back with one hand. He always did that to his hair when he was really tense.

"We told you about the Phantom this morning, but you didn't believe us."

"Of course I didn't believe you!" Ms. Walker declared. "It's an old legend. Just a story." She frowned at Zeke.

Zeke let out a frustrated sigh. "We saw the Phantom, Ms. Walker. Brooke and I. We saw him. He's the one who painted all over the backdrop. Not us. He's the one who swung down from the catwalk. And grabbed Brooke at rehearsal."

"Why should I believe that?" Ms. Walker demanded, her arms still tightly crossed in front her.

"Because it's true," I said. "Zeke, Brian, and I — we came to the auditorium to look for the Phantom."

"Where were you going to look for him?" Ms. Walker asked.

"Well," Zeke stammered. "Probably underneath the stage."

"You were going to take the trapdoor down?" Ms. Walker asked.

I nodded. "Maybe. If we had to."

"But I clearly instructed everyone to stay away from the trapdoor," she said.

"I know," I told her. "And I'm sorry. We're all sorry. But we are really desperate to find the Phantom, to prove to you that he is real, that we're not making him up."

Her expression remained hard. She continued to glare at us. "I haven't heard anything to convince me," she said.

"When we got here, we heard some noises," Zeke told her, shifting uncomfortably from foot to foot. "Footsteps. Floorboards creaking. So we knew someone else was here."

"And then the backdrop started to come down," Brian broke in, his voice shaky and small. "We just stood here and watched it, Ms. Walker. That's the truth. And then when we saw how it was messed up, we . . . we couldn't believe it!"

Ms. Walker's expression softened a little. Brian sounded so upset, I think she was starting to believe him.

"I worked so hard on that backdrop," Brian continued. "It was the first thing I ever worked on at this school, and I wanted it to be good. I wouldn't wreck my own backdrop for a dumb joke. I really wouldn't."

Ms. Walker uncrossed her arms. She glanced at each of us, then returned her eyes to the backdrop. Her lips silently formed the words of the scrawled message:

STAY AWAY FROM MY
HOME SWEET HOME

She shut her eyes and kept them shut for a long moment. Then she turned back to us. "I want to believe you," she confessed with a sigh. "But I just don't know."

She began to pace back and forth in front of us. "I drove back to school because I'd forgotten your math test papers. I heard voices in the auditorium. I come in here, and I find you on the stage. The scenery totally smeared and destroyed. The paint still wet. And you ask me to believe that a mysterious phantom from over seventy years ago is responsible."

I didn't say a word. Neither did Zeke or Brian. I don't think we had anything more to say.

"The weird thing is, I'm starting to believe you," Ms. Walker said, frowning.

The three of us let out relieved sighs.

"At least, I'm starting to believe that you didn't paint on the backdrop." She shook her hair hard. Her skinny body shuddered. "It's getting late," she said softly. "Let's all go home. I need to think about this. Maybe we need to ask Mr. Levy for an investigation. Maybe he can help us find the culprit who is trying to ruin our play."

Oh, no, I thought. *Not the principal. What if he decides to cancel our play?* But I didn't say anything. None of us did. We didn't even look at one another. We followed Ms. Walker out into the hall.

I was just so relieved that she had started to believe us. And that she was letting us go.

She clicked on a hall light so we could see our way.

We took a few steps, walking behind her.

Then we all stopped at once.

We all saw the red paint spots on the hall floor. A trail of red paint spots.

"Well, look at this!" Ms. Walker declared. "Our painter was a little careless. He or she left a trail to follow."

She clicked on more lights.

We followed the red paint splotches down the long hall. We could clearly see a shoe print in one of the bigger paint puddles.

"I don't believe this!" Zeke whispered to me. "Someone left a trail."

"I'm glad," I whispered back. "Maybe the paint drips will lead us to the one who splotched up the backdrop."

"You mean the Phantom?" Zeke whispered.

We turned a corner. We passed a small paint smear.

"At least this will prove to Ms. Walker that we're telling the truth," Brian said softly.

We turned another corner.

The paint trail stopped suddenly. One last tiny red puddle stood in front of a locker.

"Hmmmm," Ms. Walker said thoughtfully, moving her eyes from the paint smear to the locker. "The trail seems to lead right to here."

"Hey!" Zeke cried out, startling all of us. I could see his eyes go wide with shock. "That's *my* locker!"

No one said anything for a moment.

I could hear Zeke's breaths, short and fast. I turned to him. He was staring at his locker, staring hard at the gray metal door as if he could see inside.

"Open your locker, Zeke," Ms. Walker instructed. She said it through gritted teeth.

"Huh?" Zeke gaped at her as if he didn't understand what she meant. He lowered his eyes to the smear of red paint on the floor under his locker door.

"Go ahead. Open your locker," Ms. Walker repeated patiently. She suddenly looked very tired.

Zeke hesitated. "But there's nothing in there," he protested. "Just books and notebooks and stuff."

"Please." Ms. Walker motioned to the combination lock with one hand. "Please, Zeke. It's really late."

"But you don't think —?" Zeke started.

Ms. Walker motioned to the lock again.

"Maybe somebody wanted to make it look like Zeke was the one with the paint," I suggested. "Maybe someone deliberately made that trail of paint lead to Zeke's locker."

"Maybe," Ms. Walker replied calmly. "That's why I want him to open his locker."

"Okay, okay," Zeke muttered. His hand shook as he reached for the combination lock. He leaned his head forward and concentrated as he spun the dial, first one direction, then the other.

"Give me some light," he said edgily.

I backed up. "Sorry." I didn't realize I was standing in his light.

I glanced at Brian. He had his hands shoved in his pockets. He leaned against the wall and stared intently at Zeke's hands as Zeke twirled the lock.

Finally, Zeke pulled the lock open with a loud *click*.

He lifted the handle and pulled open the door.

I leaned forward to peer inside at the same time as Ms. Walker. We nearly bumped heads.

We both saw the can of paint at the same time.

A small can of red paint resting on the locker floor.

The lid wasn't on tight. Splashes of red paint dripped over the side of the can.

"But it isn't *mine*!" Zeke wailed.

Ms. Walker let out a long sigh. "I'm sorry, Zeke."

"It isn't mine!" Zeke whined. "Really, Ms. Walker! It *isn't*!"

"I'm going to call your parents to come in for a serious talk," Ms. Walker said, biting her lower lip. "And, of course, you're out of the play."

"Oh, nooo!" Zeke moaned. He slammed the locker door shut as hard as he could. The crash echoed down the long, empty hall.

Ms. Walker flinched from the sound. She flashed Zeke an angry look. Then she turned to Brian and me. "So you two were also involved? Tell the truth!"

"No!" Brian and I both called out. "We didn't do it," I added. I started to say, "Neither did Zeke."

But I could see that it was too late. There was no way to argue against the can of paint in the locker.

Zeke was a cooked goose.

"If I find out that you and Brian had anything to do with it, I'll remove you from the play and call your parents in, too," Ms. Walker threatened. "Now go home. All of you."

We turned and trudged out the door without another word.

The night air felt cold against my hot skin. I shivered.

The half-moon was covered by a sheet of gray mist. The mist looked like a ghostly figure floating over the moon.

I followed Zeke and Brian down the concrete steps. A gust of wind made my jacket flap behind me.

"Do you believe it?" Zeke muttered angrily. "Do you believe it?"

"No," I replied, shaking my head. Poor Zeke. I could see he was really messed up. And when his parents got that call from Ms. Walker, Zeke was going to be even *more* messed up!

"How did that paint get in your locker?" Brian asked him, his eyes peering into Zeke's.

Zeke turned away. "How should I know?" he snapped.

We made our way to the sidewalk. Zeke angrily kicked an empty cardboard juice box into the street.

"See you tomorrow, I guess," Brian said unhappily. He gave us a little wave, then turned and started walking slowly toward his house.

Zeke jogged off in the other direction.

"Aren't you going to walk home with me?" I called.

"No," he shouted back, and kept going.

In a way I was glad he had left. I didn't really know what to say to him.

I just felt so bad.

I started walking slowly, my head down, thinking hard, when I saw a small, round light floating toward me through the darkness.

The light grew bigger. I realized it was a bicycle headlight. The bike turned out of the school parking lot and rolled smoothly, steadily toward me.

When it was a few feet away, I recognized the bike rider. "Tina!" I cried in surprise. "What are *you* doing here?"

She squealed to a stop, bouncing in the seat. Her dark eyes caught the light of the streetlamp above us. She smiled. An odd smile.

"Hi, Brooke. How's it going?" she asked.

Was she in the school? I wondered. *Did she just come out of the school?*

"Where'd you come from?" I repeated.

Her strange smile remained on her face. "A friend's," she said. "I'm just coming from a friend's."

"Were you in the school?" I blurted out.

"The school? No. Not me," she replied. She shifted her weight, then raised her feet to the pedals. "Better zip up that jacket, Brooke," she said. "You don't want to catch a cold, do you?"

On Saturday we had play rehearsals all day long in the auditorium. The performance was only a week away.

We all worked hard, and the rehearsal went well. I only forgot my lines twice.

But it wasn't the same without Zeke.

Robert Hernandez had taken Zeke's place. I like Robert, but he's a very serious guy. He doesn't get my jokes, and he doesn't like to kid around or be kidded.

After lunch, Robert and Corey were rehearsing a scene together. Ms. Walker still hadn't returned from lunch.

I wandered over to Brian. He had a paintbrush in his hand, dripping with black paint. He was leaning over the new backdrop, putting some final touches on the gray bricks.

"Looks good," I told him. I had a sudden urge to slap him on the back and make him smear black paint all over. But I decided that might not go over too well.

I don't know *where* these sudden urges come from.

"How's it going?" Brian asked without looking up. He was filling in some spots he had missed.

"Okay, I guess," I replied. Across the stage, I saw Tina working with a large glue pot. She was brushing a thick layer of glue onto a cardboard chandelier.

"Robert is going to be a good Phantom," Brian said, scratching his chin with the tip of the paint-brush handle.

"Yeah," I agreed. "But I kind of miss Zeke."

Brian nodded. Then he turned to look up at me. "You know what? There hasn't been one practical joke since Zeke left. No scenery ruined. No mysterious phantoms leaping out at us. No threatening words scrawled on the walls. Nothing. Nothing bad since Ms. Walker kicked Zeke out."

I hadn't thought about it until that second. But Brian was right. Ever since Zeke had been removed from the play, the Phantom had totally disappeared.

Everything had been going so smoothly. I hadn't even stopped to realize it.

Did this mean that Zeke actually was the Phantom? That Zeke had been doing all those horrible things after all?

"Did Zeke's parents have a cow when Ms. Walker called them in to school?" Brian asked. "Did he get punished?"

"For sure," I replied, still thinking about the Phantom. "His parents grounded him for life. And no horror movies. Zeke can't *live* without horror movies!"

Brian snickered. "Maybe Zeke has seen *too many* horror movies," he said.

"Okay, people!" a voice called loudly. I turned to see that Ms. Walker had returned from lunch. "Let's take it from the opening of Act Two," she called. "We'll do the whole act."

I said good-bye to Brian and hurried to the front of the stage. Esmerelda was in just about every scene of Act Two. This time, I was determined to remember every word.

As I stepped beside Robert, I saw Ms. Walker pick up her script from the table where she always left it. She grasped it in both hands and started to open it to Act Two.

I watched her expression change as her hands worked at the script. She let out a short, angry cry. Then she tugged some more at the thick script.

"Hey —" she shouted angrily. "Now who's the joker?"

"Ms. Walker, what's wrong?" Robert called.

She raised the script and shook it furiously. "The pages of my script — they've all been glued together!" she fumed.

Startled gasps rose up around the stage.

"That's *it*!" Ms. Walker cried. She heaved the script at the wall. "That was the last joke! The play is canceled! Everybody go home! It's canceled."

"Did Ms. Walker change her mind?" Zeke asked.

I nodded. "Yeah. She calmed down after a few seconds and said the play could go on. But she was in a really bad mood for the rest of the day."

"At least this time she couldn't blame me," Zeke said quietly. He tossed a pink rubber ball across the living room, and Buster, his black cocker spaniel, went scrambling after it.

Brian and I had dropped by Zeke's house to tell him how things were going. Zeke was grounded — probably forever — and couldn't leave the house. His parents were at the movies. They'd be home in a few hours.

Buster dropped the ball and started barking at Brian.

Zeke laughed. "He doesn't like you, Brian." He picked up the ball and bounced it over the carpet again.

But Buster ignored the ball and kept barking at Brian.

Brian blushed. He reached out to pet the dog's head. "What's your problem, fella? I'm not a bad guy."

Buster scampered away from Brian and crossed the room to search for the ball, which had rolled into the hallway.

"Well, I guess this proves there's some other joker in the class," Zeke said, his smile fading. He settled back on the couch. "Guess this proves that it wasn't me doing all the bad things."

I started to make a joke, but I caught the serious expression on Zeke's face. So I didn't say anything.

"There's a phantom, and it isn't me," Zeke said. "And now everyone thinks I'm a liar. Ms. Walker thinks I tried to ruin the play. Even my parents think I've turned into a bad guy."

"You were a much better Phantom than Robert," I said, trying to cheer him up. "There's less than a week to go, and Robert still keeps messing up his lines. He says he's sorry he tried out for the play. He doesn't even want to be in it now."

Zeke jumped to his feet. "If we could prove that I'm not the Phantom, I'll bet Ms. Walker would give the part back to me."

"Uh-oh," I said. I could see Zeke's mind working. I knew what he was going to say next.

"Uh-oh," Brian echoed. He also knew what Zeke was going to say.

"Let's go to school," Zeke said, his eyes wide with excitement. "Let's find the Phantom this time. I really want to get my part back."

I shook my head. "No way, Zeke —" I started.

"I really want to show everyone that I didn't try to ruin the play," Zeke insisted.

Brian tossed the ball to the dog. The dog watched it bounce away. "But you're grounded, remember?" Brian said to Zeke.

Zeke shrugged. "If we find the Phantom and prove that I'm innocent, my parents will be glad I went. And I won't be grounded anymore. Come on, guys. One more try. Please?"

I stared back at Zeke, thinking hard. I didn't think it was a good idea. The last time we sneaked into the auditorium, we ended up in major trouble.

I could see by Brian's expression that he didn't want to go, either.

But how could we say no to Zeke? He was practically begging us!

It was a warm night, but I felt chilled just the same. As we walked to school, I kept seeing shadows moving close as if reaching for us. But when I turned to see them, they vanished.

Brooke, you have too much imagination, I scolded myself.

I wished my heart would stop thudding like a bass drum.

I wished I were home, watching TV with Jeremy. I had a bad feeling about our little adventure. A very bad feeling.

We didn't waste any time trying the doors. We climbed into school through the same home ec room window. Then, once again we made our way silently down the dark halls to the auditorium.

One row of lights had been left on at the back of the seats. The stage lay dark and bare, except for the gray brick backdrop against the back wall.

Zeke led the way down the center aisle. He had given us each a flashlight. We clicked them on as we made our way to the stage. The beams of light played over the empty rows of seats. I raised mine to the stage and swept it from side to side.

No one up there. No sign of anything unusual.

"Zeke, this is a waste of time," I said, whispering even though no one could hear us.

He raised a finger to his lips. "We're going down below the stage," Zeke said quietly, his eyes straight ahead. "And we're going to find him, Brooke. This time, we're going to find him."

I had never seen Zeke so serious, so determined. A chill of fear went slowly down my back. But I decided not to argue with him.

"Uh . . . maybe I should stay up on the stage while you two go down," Brian suggested. "I could stand guard."

"Stand guard against what?" Zeke demanded, raising his flashlight to Brian's face.

I could see Brian's frightened expression. "Against . . . anyone who might come," he replied weakly.

"All three of us have to go down," Zeke insisted. "If we do find the Phantom, I want two witnesses — you and Brooke."

"But the Phantom is a *ghost* — right?" Brian demanded. "How do we find a ghost?"

Zeke glared at him. "We'll find him."

Brian shrugged. We could both see that there was no point in arguing with Zeke tonight.

The floorboards on the stage creaked as we made our way to the trapdoor. Our flashlights moved over the outline of the square platform in the floor.

Brian and I huddled close together in the center of the square. Zeke stomped hard on the little wooden peg, then jumped beside us.

We heard the familiar clanking sound. Then the gentle hum as the platform started to lower. The stage appeared to rise up all around us. In a few seconds, we were surrounded by four black walls.

The light from our flashlights washed over the walls as we sank lower and lower under the stage. My heart felt as if it were sinking, too — down to my knees!

The three of us stood pressed together in the center of the platform. The clanking and grinding sounds grew louder as we went down. Finally, we hit the bottom with a hard *thud*.

For a few seconds, none of us moved.

Zeke was the first to step off the platform. He raised his flashlight and swept it slowly around. We were in the middle of a large, empty chamber. It tunneled out in two directions.

"Here, Phantom! Here, boy!" Zeke called softly, as if calling his dog. "Here, Phantom. Where *are* you, Phantom?" he called in a singsong voice.

I stepped off the platform and gave him a shove. "Stop it," I insisted. "I thought you were serious about this. Why are you making a joke of it?"

"Just trying to keep you from getting too scared," Zeke replied. But, of course, I knew the truth. He was trying to keep *himself* from getting too scared.

I turned back to Brian. In the dim light, he looked scared enough for both of us! "There's no one down here. Can we go back up now?" he pleaded.

"No way," Zeke told him. "Follow me. Keep your light down on the ground so we can see where we're going."

Walking side by side, Brian and I followed Zeke into the chamber. We stepped into a long tunnel, took a few steps, then stopped to listen.

Silence.

My legs were trembling. In fact, my entire body was shaking. But Zeke was acting so brave. There was no way I'd let him know how frightened I was.

"This tunnel probably stretches all the way under the school," Zeke whispered, moving his light ahead of us. "Maybe even farther. Maybe it goes under the entire block!"

We took another few steps — then stopped when we heard a noise behind us.

A clanking, followed by a loud hum.

"Hey!" Brian cried out shrilly. "The trapdoor!"

All three of us spun around and started running back toward it. Our heavy footsteps echoed loudly through the dark tunnel.

My chest was aching so hard by the time we got back to the trapdoor platform, I could hardly breathe.

"It — it's going back up!" Zeke cried.

We stood there helplessly, gazing at the platform as it rose over our heads, climbing back up to the stage.

"Push the switch!" Zeke cried to me. "Bring it back down!"

I fumbled on the wall till I found the switch. I tried to move it. But it was stuck.

No. It had been locked.

It wouldn't budge.

The trapdoor platform stopped high above us. A heavy silence fell over the three of us as we stared up in the darkness.

"Zeke, now we're trapped down here," I uttered. "There's no way back up. We're totally trapped."

We waited to see if someone was coming down. But the trapdoor remained closed up there.

Brian let out a frightened sigh. "Somebody did it," he whispered, staring up to the platform. "Somebody pushed the switch and sent it back up."

"The Phantom!" I cried. I turned to Zeke. "Now what?"

Zeke shrugged. "Now we have no choice. If we want to get *out* of here, we *have* to find the Phantom!"

Our circles of yellow light trembled over the floor as we turned and headed back into the tunnel. No one said a word as we followed it around one curve, then another.

The floor became soft and muddy. The air grew cooler.

I heard a soft chittering sound in the distance. I hoped it wasn't a bat.

Brian and I had to hurry to keep up with Zeke. He was taking long strides, his flashlight swinging back and forth in front of him.

Suddenly, I heard a low, musical humming. It took me a while to realize it was coming from Zeke. He was humming a tune to himself.

Come on, Zeke, give me a break! I thought. *You've got to be scared! You can't fool me with a little cheerful humming. You are as scared as I am!*

I started to tease him about it. But the tunnel suddenly ended, and we found ourselves at a low doorway. Brian hung back. But Zeke and I stepped up to the door, our flashlights beaming over it.

"Anyone in there?" Zeke called in a strange, tiny voice.

No reply.

I reached out and pushed the door. It creaked open. Zeke and I raised our flashlights and aimed them inside.

A room. All furnished. I saw a folding chair. A beat-up couch with one of the cushions missing. Bookshelves along one wall.

My flashlight fell over a small table. A bowl and a box of cornflakes stood on the table. I swept the light around and saw a small unmade bed against the far wall.

Zeke and Brian followed me into the room. Our beams of light slid slowly over every object, every piece of furniture. An old-fashioned record player stood on a low table. A stack of old records was piled beside it.

"Do you *believe* this?" Zeke whispered. A grin spread over his face.

"I think we've found the Phantom's home," I whispered back.

His flashlight tilting in front of him, Brian made his way to the table. He peered down at the cereal bowl. "The Phantom — he was just here," Brian said. "The cereal isn't soggy yet."

"This is amazing!" I cried. "Someone actually lives down here, way below the —"

I stopped because I felt a sneeze coming on. Maybe a whole sneezing fit.

I tried to hold it in. But I couldn't. I sneezed once. Twice. Five times.

"Stop it, Brooke!" Brian pleaded. "He'll *hear* you!"

"But we *want* to find him," Zeke reminded Brian.

I sneezed seven times. Then one more for good luck. Finally, I was all sneezed out.

"He heard that. I *know* he did," Brian fretted. His eyes darted around in fear.

The door slammed shut.

"Nooo!" We all jumped and cried out.

My heart leaped to my mouth. Every muscle in my body tied itself into a knot.

We turned to stare at the door. Someone had closed it, I knew. It hadn't been blown shut by any wind.

Zeke was the first to move. Lowering his flashlight, he hurtled to the door. He grabbed the knob and pushed hard.

The door didn't budge.

Zeke lowered his shoulder against the door. Twisting the knob, he pushed again.

Still no success.

He banged his shoulder against the door. Pushed again. Strained against the door with all his weight.

When he turned back to us, his face revealed his fear for the first time. "We — we're locked in," he said softly.

I rushed up beside Zeke. "Maybe if all three of us try," I suggested.

"Maybe," Zeke replied. But I could see he didn't have much hope.

I swallowed hard. Seeing Zeke so frightened made me even *more* frightened.

"Yeah. Let's all push together," Brian agreed, stepping up beside me. "We can *break* the door down if we have to."

Way to go, Brian! I thought. *He's finally showing some spirit.*

We lined up against the door and prepared to push.

I took a deep breath and held it. I was trying to calm myself down. My arms and legs felt as if they were made of chewing gum.

This is just so scary, I realized. *If we are locked in this tiny room and can't get out, we could be here for the rest of our lives. We are miles and miles away from the rest of the world.*

Everyone will search and search up above. And they'll never find us. And even if we yell and scream at the tops of our lungs for help, there's no way anyone could hear us.

We'll be trapped here forever.

I took another deep breath. "Okay, on the count of three," I said. "On three, everybody push."

Zeke started to count. "One . . . two . . ."

"Whoa! Wait a minute!" I interrupted. I stared at the door. "We pushed the door to get in here — right?"

"Yeah, I guess," Zeke replied, staring hard at me.

"So it won't *push* open from the inside," I said. "We have to *pull* it open."

"Hey — you're right!" Zeke cried.

I grabbed the knob, twisted it, and pulled hard. The door slid open easily.

And there was a man standing in the doorway.

My flashlight moved up to his face. I recognized him instantly.

Emile. The little white-haired man who said he was the night janitor.

He blocked the doorway and glared in at us, an ugly, menacing scowl on his scarred face.

"Let us go!" I shrieked.

He didn't move. His strange gray eyes moved from Zeke to Brian to me.

"You have to let us out of here!" I insisted. And then I added meekly, "Please?"

His scowl grew even angrier. The light from the flashlight made the long scar on his cheek look even deeper.

He didn't budge from the doorway. "Why are you down here?" he demanded in his hoarse whisper of a voice. "Why are you in my home?"

"So — you *are* the Phantom!" I blurted out.

He narrowed his eyes at me in surprise. "Phantom?" His expression turned thoughtful. "I guess you could call me that."

Brian uttered a low cry.

"This is my home sweet home," the man said angrily. "Why are you here? Why didn't you listen to my warnings?"

"Your warnings?" I asked. I was shaking so hard, the light from my flashlight was dancing all over the wall.

"I did everything I could to keep you away," the Phantom said. "To keep you from my home."

"You mean the paint on the backdrop? Swinging down from the catwalk? The scary mask in my locker with the note?" I cried in astonishment.

The Phantom nodded. "I tried to warn you. I didn't want to hurt anyone. But I had to protect my home."

"And so you tried to stop our play?" Zeke demanded, huddling close to me. "You tried to ruin our play so we wouldn't use the trapdoor and find you down here?"

The Phantom nodded.

"And what happened seventy-two years ago?" I asked him. "What happened to you the first time the play was supposed to be performed? Why did you disappear that night?"

The Phantom's expression changed. I saw confusion in his silvery eyes. "I — I don't understand," he stammered, staring hard at me, his white hair falling over his forehead.

"Seventy-two years ago," I insisted.

A bitter smile formed on his lips. "Hey, I'm not *that* old!" he replied. "I'm only fifty-seven."

"Then . . . you're not the Phantom?" Zeke asked uncertainly.

Emile shook his head. He let out a weary sigh. "I don't understand this Phantom talk, young man. I'm just a poor homeless guy trying to protect my little space."

All three of us studied him, trying to decide if he was telling the truth. I decided that he was. "You've been living here under the school?" I asked softly. "How did you know about this room down here?"

"My father worked at the school for thirty years," Emile replied. "He used to bring me here with him when I was a kid. When I lost my apartment in town, I remembered this space. I've been living here ever since. For nearly six months now."

His eyes glared angrily again. He brushed the hair off his forehead as his ugly scowl returned. "But you're ruining it for me, aren't you?" he said sharply. "You're ruining it all for me."

He moved quickly, stepping from the doorway, entering the room, walking toward us with that menacing expression.

I stumbled back. "Wh-what are you going to do to us?" I cried.

"You ruined everything. Everything," he repeated, moving toward us.

"Now, wait —" I cried, raising my hands as if to shield myself.

Then I heard a sound. From out in the tunnel. A low clanking sound.

I turned to Zeke and Brian. They heard it, too.

The trapdoor! It was moving. Coming down. We could hear it at the other end of the tunnel.

I think all three of us had the same idea at once. We *had* to get to that trapdoor. It was our only chance of escape.

"You ruined everything," Emile repeated, suddenly sounding more sad than angry. "Why didn't you listen to my warnings?"

Without saying a word to each other, Zeke, Brian, and I charged for the door. "Oh!" I bumped into Emile as I scooted past.

To my surprise, he didn't reach out to grab me, didn't try to stop me.

I led the way out the door, running at full speed. My legs still felt as rubbery as chewing gum. But I forced them to move. One running step, then another.

I didn't glance back. But I could hear Zeke and Brian at my heels. And then I heard Emile's voice echoing through the tunnels: "You ruined everything. Everything!"

Was Emile chasing after us?

I didn't care. I just wanted to get to the trapdoor platform and get out of there!

I plunged blindly through the dark, curving tunnel. My sneakers sank into the soft dirt floor as I ran. My shoulder scraped the rough wall, but I didn't slow down.

The light bounced over the ground at my feet. I raised it as the trapdoor platform came into view. I was gasping for breath. My side ached from running.

"Huh? What are *you* doing down here?" a man's voice called.

Zeke's dad!

Zeke, Brian, and I scrambled onto the platform, squeezing beside him.

"What's going on?" Mr. Matthews demanded. "Whose voice is that?"

"Up!" I managed to choke out. "Take us up."

Zeke reached out and flipped the switch. This time it moved.

With a hard jerk, the platform started to raise itself.

I gazed back to the tunnel. Had Emile followed after us?

No. No sign of him.

He hadn't even chased us.

Weird, I thought. *So weird.*

"I heard a man's voice. Who was that?" Mr. Matthews demanded again.

"A homeless guy. Living beneath the stage," I said, and explained what had happened and how he had been trying to scare us for weeks.

"How did you know we were down there?" Zeke asked his dad.

"You were supposed to be at home," he replied sternly. "You were grounded. You're *still* grounded. But when you weren't at home, I figured I'd find you poking around the stage again. The side door to the school was open. I entered the auditorium and heard the trapdoor moving. I decided to see what was going on."

"I'm so glad!" I cried. I felt like hugging Mr. Matthews.

As soon as the platform stopped, we scrambled onto the stage. Zeke's dad hurried to call the police. He told them there was a homeless guy living under the school.

The police arrived quickly. We watched them go down the trapdoor. We waited for them to bring Emile up. But they returned a few minutes later without him.

"No one down there," an officer reported. He removed his helmet and scratched his wavy black hair. "No sign of anyone, either. Just a bed and some old furniture."

"What about his food? His books?" I asked.

"All gone," the officer replied. "Guess he cleared out real fast. The basement door was still slightly open."

After the police left, Brian said good night and headed out of the auditorium. Zeke's dad was going to drive me home.

I turned to Zeke. "So, there's your Phantom," I said with a little sadness. "Just a poor homeless man. Not a seventy-two-year-old ghost who's been haunting the school since it was built. Just a poor homeless man."

"Yeah, it's disappointing," Zeke replied, frowning. "I really wanted to meet a real ghost, a real phantom." His expression brightened. "But at least now Ms. Walker will believe me. And I'll get my part in the play back."

The play. I'd almost forgotten about the play.

Zeke was right, I thought happily. *He'll get his part back now. Everything will go fine.*

The Phantom is gone.

Now we can all relax, I thought. *Now we can enjoy ourselves and put on a great performance.*

Wow. Was I wrong!

The night of the performance, I sat in the girls' dressing room, smearing globs of stage makeup all over my face. I'd never worn so much makeup before and didn't think I was doing it right. I didn't even want to wear the gunk in the first place.

But Ms. Walker said we all had to. Even the guys. She said it cuts down on the glare from the lights and makes your face less shiny onstage.

It was a wild scene in the girls' dressing room. We were all struggling into our costumes and brushing on makeup. Lisa Rego and Gia Bentley — two fifth-graders who didn't even have big parts in the play — were hogging the full-length mirror, laughing and giggling and admiring themselves.

By the time I got to check myself out, the stage manager was calling, "Places! Places, everyone!"

My stomach jumped. *Calm down, Brooke*, I ordered myself. *This is supposed to be fun — remember?*

I stepped out of the dressing room, crossed the hall, entered the auditorium through the stage door, and took my place at the side of the stage. Someone tapped me on the shoulder, and I jumped a mile. Man, was I jittery!

I whirled around and found myself face-to-face with the Phantom!

I knew it was Zeke in his costume and mask, but he startled me just the same. "Zeke! You look so *real*! You look awesome!" I told him.

Zeke didn't reply. He gave me a very formal bow from the waist, then hurried to take his place.

The curtain was closed. But I could hear the steady rumble of voices out in the auditorium. I peeked out of the side of the curtain. Wow! Every seat was filled. That thought sent my stomach doing jumping jacks all over again.

The lights began to dim. The audience instantly became silent. The stage lights went up. The music started.

Go for it, Brooke, I told myself. *Just go for it!*

The play didn't get strange until the end of the first act. We were all doing really well until then.

When the curtain opened, and the audience applauded the set, I stepped out onstage with Corey. And I completely forgot about my stage fright.

"Be careful, daughter," Corey warned, playing my father. "There's a creature living beneath this theater. A twisted phantom, scarred and ugly."

"I do not believe you, Father," I replied as Esmerelda. "You are only trying to control me, to keep me a child!"

The audience seemed to be having a great time. They laughed in the right places and applauded several times.

This is excellent*!* I thought. I was excited without being nervous. I was enjoying every minute of the performance.

And as the first act drew near its end, I knew the real highlight of the show was coming. A fog of dry ice swept slowly over the stage. Blue lights swirled through the twisting fog, making it appear eerie and unreal.

I heard the clank of the trapdoor. I knew it was carrying Zeke in his Phantom costume up from down below.

In seconds, the Phantom would make his big entrance, rising up in the blue fog.

The audience will love it, I thought, watching the fog billow up over my long yellow dress.

"Phantom, is that you?" I called. "Are you coming to see me?"

The Phantom's blue-and-green mask floated up in the fog. Then his black-caped shoulders hovered into view.

The audience gasped and then cheered as the Phantom rose, standing stiffly in the fog, his black cape billowing out behind him.

And then he stepped toward me, walking slowly, majestically.

"Oh, Phantom! We are together at last!" I cried with all the emotion I could put into it. "I have dreamed of this moment for so long!"

I took his gloved hand and led him through the swirls of blue fog to the front of the stage.

A white spotlight captured us both.

I turned to face him. Stared into his eyes behind the blue-and-green mask.

And realized instantly that it wasn't Zeke!

I started to cry out. But he squeezed my hand.

His eyes burned into mine. He seemed to be begging me with his eyes, begging me not to say anything, not to give him away.

Who is *he?* I wondered, frozen in the bright spotlight. *Why does he look familiar?*

I turned back to the audience. Silent. Waiting for me to speak.

I took a deep breath and said Esmerelda's next line. "Phantom, why do you haunt this theater? Please tell me your story. I will not be afraid."

The Phantom swept his cape behind me. His eyes were still locked on mine. His gloved hand still squeezed mine tightly, as if to keep me from escaping.

"I have lived under this theater for more than seventy years," he declared. "My story is a sad one. You might even call it tragic, my fair Esmerelda."

"Please continue!" I exclaimed.

Who is he? I asked myself. *Who?*

"I was chosen to star in a play," the Phantom revealed. "A play in this very theater. It was to be the greatest night of my life!"

He paused to take a long, deep breath.

My heart skipped a beat. *He isn't reciting the script,* I realized. *Those aren't the right words.*

What is he saying?

"But my great night was never to be!" the Phantom continued, still gripping my hand. "You see, my dear Esmerelda, an hour before the play was to begin, I fell. I plunged to my death!"

I gasped. He was pointing to the trapdoor.

I realized who he was now. He was the boy who had disappeared. The boy, seventy-two years ago, who was to star as the Phantom. But disappeared and was never found.

Here he was, standing beside me on the same stage. Here he was, revealing to us all how he had disappeared, why the play was never performed.

"There!" he cried, pointing to the opening in the stage floor. "That's where I fell! There! I fell to my death. I became a real phantom. And I've waited down there ever since, waiting, waiting. Hoping for a night like tonight when I could finally play my greatest role!"

As he finished this speech, the audience burst into cheers and loud applause.

They think it's part of the play, I realized. *They don't know the true pain behind his words.*

120

They don't know that he's revealing his true story to them.

The Phantom took a deep bow. The applause grew even louder.

The fog billowed over us both.

Who is he? Who?

The question repeated in my mind.

I had to know the answer. I had to know who the Phantom was.

As he stood up from his bow, I pulled my hand free of his.

Then I reached up — and tugged off his mask!

I squinted into the thick blue fog, desperate to see his face.

The bright spotlight flashed in my eyes, blinding me for a moment.

In that moment, the Phantom covered his face with both his hands.

I reached to pull away his hands.

"No!" he screamed. "No — you can't!"

He staggered back, away from me.

Staggered and lost his balance.

"No! No!" he cried. "You can't! You can't!"

And toppled backward.

Into the open trapdoor.

And vanished in the swirling blue fog.

I heard his scream all the way down.

Then silence.

A horrible, still silence.

The audience rose to its feet and burst into loud applause and cries of "Bravo!"

They all thought it was part of the play.

But I knew better. I knew that the Phantom had finally revealed himself after seventy-two years. That he had finally had his moment on the stage.

And that he had died all over again.

As the curtain closed, muffling the excited cheers of the audience, I stood at the opening in the floor, my hands pressed to my face.

I couldn't speak. I couldn't move.

I stared down into the hole in the floor and saw only blackness.

Then, raising my eyes, I saw Zeke running across the stage to me. Wearing jeans and a white T-shirt, he lurched toward me, his expression dazed.

"Zeke!" I cried.

"Ow. Someone hit me, I think," he moaned, rubbing the back of his head. "I've been out cold." He raised his eyes to mine. "Brooke, are you okay? Did —?"

"The Phantom!" I cried. "He took your part, Zeke. He — he's down there!" I pointed into the opening. "We've got to find him!"

I stepped on the peg. The trapdoor clanked and groaned. The platform returned to the top.

Zeke and I climbed aboard.

We rode it down, down to the dark chamber below.

We searched every corner. We didn't find him.

We didn't find the mask. Or the costume. Or anything.

Somehow I knew we wouldn't.

Somehow I knew we would never see him again.

"Great job, people! Great job!" Ms. Walker called to us as we trooped offstage. "Phantom, I like the new lines you added! Great job! See you all at the cast party!"

Zeke and I struggled to get to the dressing room so we could get changed. But we were mobbed by people who wanted to congratulate us and tell us how talented and terrific we were.

The play was a major success!

I searched for Brian. I wanted to tell him all about the Phantom. But I couldn't see him in the excited crowd of friends and parents.

"Come on — let's get out of here!" Zeke cried. He pulled me by the hand out of the auditorium and into the hall.

"Wow! We're a hit!" I exclaimed, feeling totally wrecked and pumped and dazed and crazed, all at the same time. "Good thing you were able to change into the spare Phantom costume before the second act!"

"Let's just get our coats and get changed at home," Zeke suggested. "We can try to figure out who played my part on the way. Then we can meet at my house to go to the party."

"Okay," I agreed. "But we have to hurry. My parents are waiting to tell me what a fabulous star I am!"

The sound of excited chattering and laughter drifted from the auditorium and followed us as we made our way to our lockers.

"Hey —" I stopped in front of my locker. "Look, Zeke — the door is open. I didn't leave it unlocked."

"Weird," Zeke murmured.

I pulled the door all the way open, and a book toppled out onto the floor.

I bent to pick it up. It was an old book, its brown cover worn and dusty. I turned it around, squinting to read the cover in the dim hall light.

"It's a really old yearbook," I told Zeke. "Look. It's from this school. Woods Mill. But it's from the 1930s."

"Huh? How'd it get in your locker?" Zeke asked, staring down at it.

My eyes fell on a torn sheet of paper tucked inside. A bookmark.

Gripping the old heavy book in both hands, I opened to the pages marked by the bookmark.

"Wow!" Zeke cried. "I don't believe it!"

We were staring at a yearbook article about the play we had just performed. THE PHANTOM TO BE PERFORMED IN THE SPRING, read the headline at the top.

"This must have been written early that school year," I said. "We know the play was never performed. We know the whole story of what happened back then."

"Hold the book up to the light," Zeke instructed. "Let's check out the pictures."

I raised the book, and we both stared down at the small photographs that covered the two pages.

Then we saw it.

A small, blurred black-and-white photo of the boy who had won the starring role, the boy who was to play the Phantom. The boy who had disappeared.

The boy was Brian.

BEHIND THE SCREAMS

PHANTOM OF THE AUDITORIUM

CONTENTS

Bonus material written and compiled
by Gabrielle S. Balkan

About the Author

R.L. Stine's books are read all over the world. So far, his books have sold more than 300 million copies, making him one of the most popular children's authors in history. Besides Goosebumps, R.L. Stine has written the teen series Fear Street, the funny series Rotten School, as well as the Mostly Ghostly series, The Nightmare Room series, and the two-book thriller *Dangerous Girls*. R.L. Stine lives in New York with his wife, Jane, and Minnie, his King Charles spaniel. You can learn more about him at www.RLStine.com.

Q & A with R.L. Stine

Have you ever participated in a school play? Are you a "spotlight hog" like Zeke or a "happy to work your magic behind the scenes" like Brian?

R.L. Stine (RLS): *I was never in the school plays, but I have been on TV. The first time I was on TV, I couldn't remember my first line. Here's the sad part. My first line was, "Hello, I'm R.L. Stine."*

Zeke dislikes his freckles and Brooke wishes to be glasses-free. Have you ever wished you could change part of your appearance?

RLS: *Well it's a real drag growing werewolf fur every full moon. . . . Just kidding. Everyone knows I'm a vampire, not a werewolf.*

How do you decide which of your books, like *Say Cheese and Die!* will have a sequel? Do you like writing follow-up stories?

RLS: *I've written the most follow-up books about Slappy, the living dummy. I did those because Slappy threatened me—you know how he is. Actually, I usually write sequels if a lot of my readers ask me to. Do you have one to suggest for me?*

Do you ever base your book ideas on current news, movies, songs, or events?

RLS: *No. Real life is too weird and scary for me! But a lot of my titles are based on titles of old horror movies.*

Goosebumps Hall of Horrors #3 Special Edition: *The Five Masks of Dr. Screem* is another epic Halloween adventure. What sets Dr. Screem apart from the other devious characters you've created?

RLS: *I can't tell you. He is a man of mystery. . . . Even I don't understand him!*

To find out R.L. Stine's favorite vampire, pick up the special collector's edition of **VAMPIRE BREATH**.

Haunted Theaters

The play space at Woods Mill Middle School is not the only theater where **STRANGE** things have been known to happen. Find out about more haunted theaters around the United States.

SINFULLY FUN

BIRD CAGE THEATRE
TOMBSTONE, ARIZONA

The Wild West is known for places like the Bird Cage Theatre, a former saloon where all sorts of gambling and rowdy behavior took place—including 26 murders! The ghosts in this establishment do very little **FRIGHTENING** and mostly continue the fun they knew in life. If you visit the Bird Cage Theatre, you will find a nineteenth-century horse-drawn hearse and 148 bullet holes in the floor and ceiling!

THE DARLING OF THE BALCONY

LANDMARK THEATRE
SYRACUSE, NEW YORK

She is known either as Claire, Clarice, or The Lady in White, and there is more than one theory about how this woman came to haunt this grand New York State theater. In one story, she fell from the mezzanine after seeing her husband electrocuted while working onstage. In another, she jumped after losing a part in a play. People claim to see her sitting quietly in the balcony from where she met her **DEMISE** and attribute cold spaces in the theater to her presence.

THE GIRL WHO WOULD NOT GROW UP

ORPHEUM THEATRE
MEMPHIS, TENNESSEE

This playhouse was made famous in part by the songs of Elvis Presley. But Memphis has another young musical talent, a girl called Mary, who makes her mark playing the organ from beyond the grave. When she is not playing "Never Never Land," Mary can be found opening and closing doors, playing **PRANKS** on the actors, or giggling over her mischief in seat C-5. We suppose if you are going to spend eternity as a tween ghost, a theater is a pretty good place to do it!

PRETTY IN PITTSBURGH

PITTSBURGH PLAYHOUSE
PITTSBURGH, PENNSYLVANIA

This century-old building was home to many different types of businesses before it became a place for plays, but it was a theater when one of its most recognizable ghosts came to be. Called Gorgeous George, this hideous specter is anything but. Known not by his ghostly origin but by his green, rotting, **PUTRID** face, George is said to sneak up on people, get their attention by tapping on their shoulders or a nearby window, and then cackle wildly once his stinking, oozing face scares them senseless.

BAD BROTHER
SPRINGER OPERA HOUSE
COLUMBUS, GEORGIA

This beautiful home of song and drama is known for the famous people who have graced its stage in life and the afterlife. In the first category we have people such as Oscar Wilde, Will Rogers, Franklin D. Roosevelt, and Edwin Booth. In the second category, we have . . . Edwin Booth! Quite famous in his day for his acting abilities, Edwin is now known for his family shame. It was Edwin's brother, John Wilkes Booth, who shot and killed President Abraham Lincoln in 1865. Now Edwin is said to **HAUNT** the Springer Opera House in a merry manner, playing backstage with the wardrobe and props.

Is Your School Haunted?

Complete these questions to find out if
your school auditorium is haunted.

At the end of every school year, the drama teacher . . .
A) is given a bouquet of roses by the graduating class.
B) quits because the acting students are such divas.
C) mysteriously disappears.

The star of the spring play . . .
A) offers to give you pointers on how to get over your
own stage fright.
B) wears sunglasses inside and is always offering to
sign your lunch bag.
C) comes to class every Monday with a new bandage on
a different part of her body.

**When a new play is announced, the librarian, who's
been at the school for 50 years, suddenly . . .**
A) displays books that have to do with the theater and
buys two tickets to the performance right away.
B) starts talking in a different accent every day:
British on Mondays, Russian on Tuesdays, etc.
C) exits the school on the side opposite from the
auditorium and takes a long vacation.

When you look up the name of your school on the Internet, you find . . .

A) a photo of the winning touchdown from last night's football game.

B) a gossipy article about the art teacher's hairdo.

C) pointers on performing exorcisms.

One afternoon, while snooping around backstage, you find . . .

A) a set of yearbooks from the year your uncle attended the same school.

B) a meeting going on behind a locked door with a sign that says, NO LOSERS ALLOWED.

C) a bucket of what looks like blood and a strange chalk pattern on the floor.

BONUS QUESTION: Does R.L. Stine go to your school, is he the principal, or is the school named after him?

If you answered mostly . . .

A's: Sorry, you are going to a completely normal school with well-adjusted teachers and students. *Boring!*

B's: Call a reality specialist—your school has been taken over by fans of celebrity TV shows.

C's: Yup, your school is haunted. You might want to consider going out for the cross-country team and leaving the acting to someone else!

The Scream of the Haunted Mask

Don't worry—this mask isn't haunted. The only scream will come from your parents if you don't get their permission before making this mask and forget to clean up afterward! This mask takes two days to make.

BEFORE YOU BEGIN, GATHER:

- aluminum foil
- plastic wrap
- masking tape
- 1 cup flour
- 1 teaspoon salt
- water
- large bowl
- newspaper
- poster or acrylic paint
- 3 feet of string

GET GOING:

1) Ask your parents to help you gather the ingredients and find a good place for you to make your haunted mask. You probably want to wear clothes you don't mind getting a little dirty.

2) Make a mold: Gently press a large piece of aluminum foil over your face.

3) Use extra foil to add details to your face mold. Pay special attention to making a revolting-looking nose, chin, and eyebrows. Maybe your mask will have warts, uneven eyebrows, or an extra eyeball!

4) Cover the foil mold with plastic wrap so the wrap clings to the foil. Use masking tape to secure the plastic wrap under the foil.

5) Make the papier-mâché: Mix the flour and salt in a bowl, adding enough water to make a thin paste. You don't want a watery paste or a goopy paste that is hard to stir.

6) Tear newspaper into ¼-inch strips. Dip the strips one at a time into the paste. Place each strip onto the foil-and-plastic-wrap mold, making sure to completely cover the mold with strips, overlapping the strips as necessary. Make two layers of newspaper strips.

7) Let the mask dry overnight. It needs to be hard and dry before you paint.

8) If your mask is dry and hard, use poster or acrylic paint to bring your hideous creation to life. Add lots of gory details like blood, oozing cuts, scars, and anything else you can think of.

9) Once your paint dries, separate the paper mask from the foil-and-plastic-wrap mold.

10) On each side of your haunted mask in the location of your ears, poke holes about ¼-inch in diameter. Cut the string in half. Tie a knot on one end of each string and run one piece through each hole.

11) Put on your mask, tie the string behind your head, and show off your creation!

The Dos and Don'ts of the Stage

Everyone knows you are supposed to say "break a leg" instead of "good luck" to someone about to go onstage, but did you know about these other strange superstitions and traditions?

NEVER SAY THE NAME OF SHAKESPEARE'S *MACBETH*. INSTEAD, ACTORS CALL IT "THE SCOTTISH PLAY."

NEVER KEEP A THEATER OPEN ALL SEVEN DAYS IN A WEEK—THE GHOSTS NEED A DAY TO PERFORM THEIR OWN PLAYS!

NEVER USE REAL MONEY—OR WEAR REAL JEWELRY—ONSTAGE.

NEVER HAVE A MIRROR ONSTAGE— BROKEN OR OTHERWISE!

NEVER ALLOW A CAT ONSTAGE DURING A PERFORMANCE, BUT KEEP ONE TO HANG AROUND DURING OTHER TIMES.

NEVER GIVE AN ACTOR FLOWERS *BEFORE* A SHOW.
AND WHEN YOU DO GIVE THEM, MAKE SURE
THEY ARE FROM A GRAVEYARD.

NEVER WEAR GREEN OR YELLOW.
AND ONLY WEAR BLUE IF YOU ARE
ALSO WEARING SILVER.

NEVER WEAR BRAND-NEW MAKEUP
ON OPENING NIGHT.

NEVER SPEAK THE LAST LINE OF A PLAY
BEFORE OPENING NIGHT.

AN ACTOR MUST NEVER WHISTLE—
ONSTAGE OR OFF.

ALWAYS KEEP AT LEAST ONE LIGHT ON
IN AN EMPTY THEATER TO GIVE GHOSTS
ENOUGH LIGHT TO SEE BY—AND KEEP THEM
FROM LASHING OUT IN ANGER!

ALWAYS EXIT THE DRESSING ROOM
WITH YOUR LEFT FOOT FIRST.

Want more chills?

Then check out

SPECIAL EDITION

THE FIVE MASKS OF DR. SCREEM

Take a peek at the all new, all-terrifying thrill ride from R.L. Stine

1

My brother, Peter, tightened the belt around his white karate uniform. "Monica," he said, "if you get more Snickers bars than me, can we trade?"

He didn't wait for me to answer.

"Mom, are we allowed to eat unwrapped candy?" he shouted. Mom was downstairs. How did he expect her to hear him?

He did a little dance and gave me a hard karate chop on the shoulder.

"*Ow*. Stop it, Peter," I groaned. I rubbed my shoulder.

He laughed. "You're such a wimp." He pretended to chop me again. I ducked away.

"Can you get dizzy from eating chocolate?" Peter asked. "Freddy Milner says if you eat enough chocolate, you get so dizzy, you can't walk straight."

"Don't try it tonight," I said.

He staggered around the room till he crashed into the wall. Then he leaped in the air and did a high karate kick.

"Look out!" I screamed. He almost kicked my laptop off the desk.

"Why don't you get out of my room and wait downstairs?" I said.

"Why don't you make me?" he said. He grinned his toothy grin as he raised both fists.

Peter thinks he's cute, but he isn't. For one thing, he's too tall to be cute. He's ten — two years younger than me — but he's nearly a foot taller than I am. He has stringy blond hair and a long, bent nose and funny teeth. He's my brother but let's face facts — he's a beast.

He picked up a postage stamp from my desk. Licked it — and stuck it to my forehead. Then he collapsed laughing on my bed.

"Why did you do that?" I growled.

He shrugged. "Why not?"

Guess you can understand why I spell Peter's name P-A-I-N.

He talks too much. He can't stand still. He's always dancing and chopping and kicking. And he thinks he's funny, but he isn't.

My friends can't stand him.

Some kids take pills to slow them down to normal speed. But my parents make excuses for Peter. They say he's just high energy.

Like I'm some kind of lazy slob. I'm only captain of the gymnastics team and star sprinter of the Hillcrest Middle School track team.

"What kind of costume is that?" Peter asked with a sneer. "A pair of black shorts over purple tights?"

"It's my gymnastics uniform," I said.

He laughed. "You look like a freak."

"Mom!" I shouted down the stairs. "Do I have to take him?"

I heard her footsteps on the stairs. I stepped out into the hall. She stopped halfway up and leaned on the banister.

"Monica, are you still complaining?" She blew back a strand of her curly copper-colored hair.

She and I have the same color hair. Actually, we kind of look like sisters. We're both small and thin. Unlike Peter and Dad, who are both gangly hulks.

I sighed. "I just want to meet up with Caroline and Regina and hang out with them."

"Well, you can't," Mom said. "You have to take Peter trick-or-treating."

I rolled my eyes. "But, Mom, all he does is practice karate on us till we're black-and-blue."

That made Peter laugh. Behind me in my room, he picked up one of my stuffed pandas and gave it some hard chops.

"You girls can defend yourselves," Mom said. "Kick him back."

Peter dropped the panda to the floor. "Huh?"

"Besides, he'll be too busy collecting candy,"

Mom said. "You know he's a total candy nut. He won't have time to pester you and your friends."

She shouted to Peter. "Am I right?"

"Whatever," Peter replied.

I sighed again. "Okay, let's get it over with," I said.

I returned to my room and pulled a silvery mask over my eyes. Maybe people wouldn't recognize me. The elastic band caught in my hair. As if being with my brother wasn't enough pain.

I turned and saw Peter pull a black mask down over his eyes. It matched the black belt around his uniform. Peter is nowhere near a black belt. But he wears one anyway.

A few seconds later, we stepped out the front door. Peter hopped down the steps and went running to the street.

It was a dark October night. A half-moon hung low over the houses across the street. The wind gusted, making dead leaves swirl in circles in the front yard.

I shivered. Maybe my shorts and tights and sleeveless T-shirt were a mistake. Maybe I needed a jacket.

But as I followed Peter away from the light of the house into the blue-black darkness, I realized I wasn't shivering from the wind.

Normally, I'm not a fraidy cat. But I just had a feeling . . .

. . . A very bad feeling about this Halloween.

2

Caroline wore a top hat, a ragged man's overcoat, big floppy shoes, and a bumpy rubber nose. She spoke in a high, creaky voice and said she was a Munchkin from *The Wizard of Oz*.

Regina wore gray spandex workout clothes. She had black whiskers painted on her cheeks. She said she was Catwoman. With her olive-colored eyes, she looked like a cat even without the whiskers.

All three of us are on the gymnastics team at school. So we are pretty strong and athletic.

But we were no match for Peter.

He kept dancing around us, making wide circles. Then he'd dart in and snatch something out of our trick-or-treat bags. He was a total thief.

"Give that back!" Regina cried. She made a grab for the candy bar Peter swiped. "That's my favorite!"

"Mine, too," Peter said, dancing away, giggling his head off. He shoved Regina's candy into his big shopping bag.

Regina didn't give up easily. She let out a roar and dove at Peter.

He dodged to the side and gave her a hard karate chop — in the neck.

"*Ullllp.*" Regina made a horrible noise and started to choke.

For once, Peter stopped dancing. "Oh. Sorry," he said. "That was an accident."

"This is an accident, too!" Caroline cried. She lowered her shoulder and plowed right into Peter.

The two of them went rolling into a pile of dry leaves. Peter held on to his trick-or-treat bag for dear life. He swung it at Caroline, and she rolled away from him.

Regina rubbed her throat. "I'm okay," she said.

"It was an accident. Really," Peter insisted. He jumped up and trotted over to Regina. He held up his shopping bag. "Take a candy. Go ahead. Take any one."

Regina eyed him suspiciously.

He shook the bag in front of her. She reached in and pulled out a big Snickers bar.

"Not *that* one!" Peter cried. He grabbed it out of her hand and backed away with it.

Regina let out a groan. "You creep!"

Caroline took Regina by the arm and started to pull her away. "Catch you later, Monica," she called.

"Hey, wait—" I started after them. "Where are you going?"

DOUBLE THE FRIGHT
ALL AT ONE SITE

www.scholastic.com/goosebumps

FIENDS OF GOOSEBUMPS & GOOSEBUMPS HORRORLAND CAN:

- PLAY GHOULISH GAMES!
- CHAT WITH FELLOW FAN-ATICS!
- WATCH CLIPS FROM SPINE-TINGLING DVDs!
- EXPLORE CLASSIC BOOKS AND NEW TERROR-IFIC TITLES!
- CHECK OUT THE GOOSEBUMPS HORRORLAND VIDEO GAME!
- GET GOOSEBUMPS PHOTOSHOCK FOR THE IPHONE™ OR IPOD TOUCH®!

SCHOLASTIC

GBWEB

Revenge of the Living Dummy
R.L. STINE
SCHOLASTIC

CREEP FROM THE DEEP
R.L. STINE
SCHOLASTIC

MONSTER BLOOD FOR BREAKFAST!
R.L. STINE
SCHOLASTIC

THE SCREAM OF THE HAUNTED MASK
R.L. STINE
SCHOLASTIC

DR. MANIAC VS. ROBBY SCHWARTZ
R.L. STINE
SCHOLASTIC

WHO'S YOUR MUMMY?
R.L. STINE
SCHOLASTIC

MY FRIENDS CALL ME MONSTER
R.L. STINE
SCHOLASTIC

SAY CHEESE - AND DIE SCREAMING!
R.L. STINE
SCHOLASTIC

WELCOME TO CAMP SLITHER
R.L. STINE
SCHOLASTIC

THE SCARIEST PLACE ON EARTH!

Goosebumps HorrorLand
HELP! WE HAVE STRANGE POWERS!
R.L. STINE

Goosebumps HorrorLand
ESCAPE FROM HORRORLAND
R.L. STINE

Goosebumps HorrorLand
THE STREETS OF PANIC PARK
R.L. STINE

Goosebumps HorrorLand
WHEN THE GHOST DOG HOWLS
R.L. STINE

Goosebumps HorrorLand
LITTLE SHOP OF HAMSTERS
R.L. STINE

Goosebumps HorrorLand
HEADS, YOU LOSE!
R.L. STINE

Goosebumps HorrorLand
WEIRDO HALLOWEEN
R.L. STINE

Goosebumps HorrorLand
THE WIZARD OF OOZE
R.L. STINE

Goosebumps HorrorLand
SLAPPY NEW YEAR!
R.L. STINE

Goosebumps HorrorLand
THE HORROR AT CHILLER HOUSE
R.L. STINE

HALL OF HORRORS—HALL OF FAME FOR THE TRULY TERRIFYING!

Goosebumps HALL OF HORRORS
CLAWS!
R.L. STINE

Goosebumps HALL OF HORRORS
NIGHT OF THE GIANT EVERYTHING
R.L. STINE

The Original Bone-Chilling

Series

—with Exclusive Author Interviews!